Lilou And the Call of The Wild:

Volume 1

Mireille Malette

DEDICATION

I dedicate this novel to my sister Lyne, thank you for your encouragement.

We all need a lucky star to guide us to move forward in the light.

Love Bé xo

THANKS

I would like to thank my three loves, Antoine, David, and Bruno.

Their love is so big that it has no words.

Thank you for being a part of my life and encouraging me;

Without you, nothing would have been possible.

And thank you to everyone who didn't believe in me,

It's thanks to you that I succeeded.

Final exams are finally over, and the allure of vacation is irresistible. Senior year in high school feels like a whole new world compared to elementary school, yet it's been a journey I've treasured. Well, maybe "treasured" is a bit much, but let's just say I really enjoyed the vibe of high school. The rotating cast of teachers for each subject kept things interesting. While I got along with all my teachers, Mr. Roy, our science guru, stood out. He's tall, young, and has this effortless charm that made him a hit with the ladies and among young, beautiful girls. Always approachable, he speaks in soothing tones, exuding a perpetual calmness that made him a go-to for post-class queries.

High school exams, especially the year-end marathon, are a universe away from the elementary league. Take French, my final exam—it was a beast. Two grueling hours of grappling with grammar, spelling, conjugations, synonyms, and antonyms, topped off with a 200-word essay on the environment. Exhausting, yes, but it's a relief to bid adieu to it all.

Tomorrow marks the bittersweet farewell to friends, some of whom we might not cross paths with during the summer break. Choices loom large as we progress through high school. In the initial year, it's a collective journey at our local comprehensive school—the only one in our vicinity. From sophomore to senior years, the options branch out. Some opt for an English-centric curriculum, others lean towards sports or technology, while a few, like me and Isabelle, stick to the familiar grounds of our neighborhood school.

Speaking of Isabelle, she's been my partner in crime since day one. Our high school saga doesn't end here; there's a sixth-year preparatory phase tailored to our career aspirations. University beckons for some, vocational paths for others, and then there are those like the Yongs, inheriting a legacy of family-run businesses like their three-generation-old convenience store. The journey from classrooms to careers awaits each of us, charting a unique course in this tapestry of high school memories.

We must also empty our lockers, bringing home everything we've brought in duplicates on occasion, like extra gym sneakers or those forgotten lunch bags. Ugh, oh my God, it does not smell great in there. But saying goodbye isn't precisely thrilling when you realize you won't see some friends again. Nathan, the charming Nathan, will attend a hockey school. He aspires to be a professional hockey player, and I'm sure he'll make it—he's among the top two in his year. But we won't see each other again because he has to move to another city. Sad. At least I will always have Isabelle with me. We're inseparable. We have lots of plans for this summer. We aim to enjoy the fireplace we built in my backyard five years ago at the onset of spring, with stones we found in the field behind my house.

We also plan to spend the entire summer sleeping outside by the fire. We want to go fishing and eat the fish we cook on our fireplace. We intend to prepare a garden to grow vegetables, do lots of biking, and especially tanning. Yes, mainly to tan while blasting our music. Isabelle and I are clearing everything out today. There's no way we're coming back tomorrow. No thanks, not one more day here, but rather an extra day on vacation. Yes, finally, vacation. Isabelle will pursue health studies next year to become a nurse. As for me, I have no clue; nothing appeals to me. I enrolled in the same course as Isabelle just to be with her. But nothing really interests me.

"Hey, hi Lilou, I wrote you a little note. Please read it only when you get home," Nathan said as he handed me a pink envelope. "I hope you have a really nice vacation." And he gave me a kiss on the cheek. I was so surprised and embarrassed that all I managed to say was...

"Okay, ...thank you."

What... The hottest guy in school comes up to give me a letter and kisses me, and all I can manage to say is, "Okay, thank you?" It is embarrassing! I just want to hide. I'm mortified.

"Come on, Lilou, what happened to you? Did you freeze on the spot or what?" Isabelle couldn't believe it.

"I didn't know what to say, and his kiss took me by surprise. Do you think I should go and talk to him?"

"He's already left in his mother's car."

"I'll call him after reading his letter."

"Will you show it to me?" Isabelle asked with a big smile.

"I'll read it first, and then we'll see."

Tucked away preciously in my backpack, the pink envelope in my French binder awaited, shielded for protection, eager to be read. I was now looking forward to getting home. What could he have possibly written to me? After emptying my locker, I quickly made the rounds of my friends to bid them farewell, wishing them a wonderful summer, wishing them to enjoy it to the fullest, and saying that we would meet again in September for the return to class. For one last year before heading off to higher studies. Isabelle followed me quietly, casting glances my way from time to time. I think she understood my dying urge to read the letter. I walked fast, nearly running. Isabelle struggled to keep up. We arrived at the corner of our street, where we lived a few houses apart.

"Bye, I'll call you later," I said before reaching her house. I lived three houses down.

"Perfect, I'll be waiting for your call," Isabelle waved, rooted at the edge of her property, watching me walk away.

I'm anxious, nervous, and not quite sure what I'm feeling—it's never happened to me before. One thing I know for sure is that I'm very eager to read what Nathan has written on that card. As I entered the house, my father was waiting in the kitchen.

"Lilou, come here, please. I need to talk to you." My father looked very serious. A slight knot formed in my stomach; I had never seen him this nervous.

"What's the matter, Dad? You don't look well. Has something happened to Maminou or Grandpa?"

"No, everything is fine, but I need to talk to you about something important. I know you won't like it, but I must tell you today. I could have told you much earlier, but I wanted you to enjoy your school years usually before bringing this up."

"You're scaring me, Dad." A huge lump formed in my stomach. I was scared. I didn't know what I was scared of, but I was afraid.

"Okay, I don't know where to start. It's nothing serious. No one is dead or injured, okay? He took a deep breath and paused... We are moving."

Silence.

***

A massive emptiness settled in my head for a few seconds. "What do you mean we are moving?"

"Have you noticed that I've been packing boxes in the attic and around the house these past few weeks?"

"Yes, I thought you wanted to clean out Stella's stuff. That it was just decluttering!"

"Well, no, we're moving in two weeks. We have to pack everything. Maminou and Grandpa came to help me today, and they'll be back tomorrow."

"No, I don't want to move. I like it here. I love my friends and my school, and I only have one year left at this school. Why do we have to leave our homes? We've always lived here. Where are we moving to?"

"To a really big house with a forest behind it. You're going to love it."

"No, I won't like it. Is it far from here?"

"Yes, it's a bit far, a few hours away, but your friends can come visit you."

"Do you really think my friends' parents will drive hours to visit me for just a few hours? No. I want to go live with Maminou, and I want to stay here."

"Maminou is moving with us, and they will live with us in the same house."

"What? Why? I don't understand anything. Why this sudden change? Isabelle and I have plans for the summer. Why didn't you tell me earlier? This isn't fair. You're being unjust. I hate you!" I yelled at my father. I ran off, taking the stairs two at a time, burst into my room, and slammed the door shut. I broke down in tears.

When I opened my eyes, my neck was sore, and I could see nothing—darkness had enveloped my room. Lying on my stomach, fully clothed, and the wrong way around in my bed, I still had my shoes on. With difficulty, I got up and sat on the edge of my bed. Stretching my neck, I glanced at the clock on my alarm: 4:00 a.m. I must have fallen asleep crying, drained. I took off my shoes, changed into pajamas, and went to the kitchen to grab a bite. My stomach was screaming with hunger. As I descended the staircase to the first floor, I caught sight of my father sleeping in the living room. I paused for a moment to watch him sleep. My last words to him had been harsh. But he had lied to me for so long. How could he?

Reaching the kitchen, I saw a note on the table. It reminded me that I hadn't read Nathan's letter in my bag. This news had turned my plans upside down. I grabbed a bowl from the cupboard, thankful my father hadn't packed it in a box while I slept. I took the milk and cereal box from the cupboard next to the fridge, opened a drawer for a spoon, and sat down at the table. Pouring the milk over my cereal, I took my first bite before unfolding the piece of paper my father had left for me.

"Dear Lilou,

I am sorry for not making the right decision earlier. I should have talked to you about this well before today. I just wanted you to have a good school year and experience your final year of high school like other teenagers. Without worries, without sadness, just normal. I realize now that it was probably the wrong decision. There are reasons, good reasons, why we need to move. I don't want to discuss this on paper; we'll talk when you wake up tomorrow. I'll be waiting in the living room in case you wake up soon, and we can talk then. I love you more than anything in the world, my dear. I hope you can forgive me."

Love, Dad.

After finishing my cereal and placing the bowl in the sink, I took a warm shower. There's nothing quite like a hot shower to help rearrange one's thoughts. I slipped into comfortable clothes—jogging pants, a hoodie, and my running shoes. I grabbed my phone and carefully descended the stairs to avoid waking my father. I wasn't ready to talk to him just yet. I needed some fresh air and time to think. I had brought along Nathan's pink envelope, which I hadn't managed to read last night as planned.

I closed the door gently behind me, not bothering with the security latch since I hadn't brought my keys for the return trip. I sauntered towards the park, aiming to sit under a tree to read Nathan's card and ponder over the news my father had shared with me yesterday. It felt like a boulder heavier than myself had crashed onto my head. Nathan had written my name on top of the envelope. His handwriting was beautiful. I tore open the envelope and pulled out a card adorned with pink roses on the cover. He knew my favorite color.

Inside was a heartfelt message from Nathan, no generic pre-written note, just his words. Fortunately, the park was almost empty at this hour, save for a man walking his leashed dog, probably to avoid the crowd, as it usually gets busy here during the day. It's a lovely park with a waterfront where one can dip their feet to cool off. Dogs sometimes plunge in, too. Geese and ducks love this place.

Well, let's read this letter.

"Hi Lilou,

I've wanted to write you this letter all year, and every day I'd tell myself, okay, tomorrow I'll have time. But I just couldn't find time for classes, studies, homework, remedial sessions, hockey practice, games, and sometimes even out of town. Hockey is very important to me, but not as much as it is to my family. My mom also nudges me to practice hockey whenever I get free. To get into the hockey school, I needed an 80% average, so I didn't have any free time to write to you, which is why I'm giving this to you today, on the last day of school. I would have loved to go to the movies with you, to sit in the park enjoying a vanilla ice cream cone."

"Or just talking while listening to music. I truly hope we'll meet this summer. Even though I have a hockey training camp, I'll still have some free time. If you feel like meeting, call me, and we can go and see a movie or take a walk. I'd really like to see you again, even if we don't attend the same school in September. I am sincerely hoping that you'll call.

XOXO.

Nathan 438-654-xxxx

I started crying. All my summer plans were falling apart, all because of a supposedly important move. I was so angry that I had a knot in my stomach that hurt. My phone rang at 5:30 a.m. Who could it have been at that time? I reached into my kangaroo pocket and checked the screen—it was my father. I didn't feel like talking to him, but he must have been wondering where I was.

"Hi, Dad."

"Lilou, where are you? I got up and saw a bowl in the kitchen sink, even though I cleaned all the dishes last night. I went up to check your room, and it was empty. I started to panic."

"Calm down, Dad, everything is fine. I just needed some air and time to think." I didn't want to tell him about the letter I was dying to read.

"Where are you?"

"At the park."

"Will you come home soon so we can talk?"

"I don't have anything to say right now. I need time; I'm too upset with you."

"But I have things to tell and explain to you."

"Well, not right now. Later. I'll probably go to Isabelle's when she wakes up." Isabelle must be wondering why I didn't call her yesterday.

"Can you please come home so we can talk?"

"No, I'm angry with you. You ruined my summer. I had plans, and now I have to tell my best friend I'm moving, and we won't see each other again. I hate you. Don't call me back. I won't answer." With that, I hung up and slipped my phone into my kangaroo pocket.

I was crying. How was I going to break it to Isabelle, my best friend, that we wouldn't see each other again because my father decided months ago that we were moving, and I had just found out today? That we wouldn't enjoy the fireplace we had built together. We wouldn't sleep under the stars, or sunbathe together, go to the movies, or see Nathan, who wanted to meet this summer. I didn't know how to tell her. I was so sad. My phone rang again. 'Maminou' was displayed on the screen. Oh Lord, Dad must have called her to say I didn't want to come home. I put my phone back in my pocket. Five minutes later, it rang again—still 'Maminou.' I answered the call.

"Maminou, I know Dad called you. I don't feel like talking to anyone right now. Can you please respect that?" I snarled. "After all, you all lied to me for months, and I am furious with everyone. Please don't bother me. I need to be alone and think."

"Okay, my dear Sylvestre, I just wanted to say I understand. I'm angry at your father, too. There hasn't been a day when I didn't tell him, 'You need to tell her right away so she can adjust.' But no, he wanted you to have a 'normal' school year like every other teenager. He wanted to wait until the last day of school to tell you everything. Now, here we are, you being angry at us all."

"Why do you and Dad keep saying that you wanted me to have a 'NORMAL' school year like all the other students? I don't understand that phrase. I didn't grasp it when Dad said it yesterday, but now that you say it too, it seems odd. Will I no longer have a normal year now that we are moving? What do you mean?"

"No, we wanted you to have a year without worrying about the move. A normal year in the sense that you wouldn't know you were leaving, a beautiful final year of high school. Because we know it's an important year for young people. You transition from the small world of elementary school to the vastness of high school. You step out of your young child's cocoon into the adolescent shell that will gradually mature into adulthood. It's a significant milestone. It's the first year you start taking responsibility for yourself, where your parents aren't looming over you as much. You make your own choices. Like your course selections, your circle of friends changes, too. And all these decisions are crucial for your future: your choices, your decisions, your future. That's why your father was so keen on giving you this year, like all other young people, so as not to disrupt your development. Given that you don't have a mother, he didn't want to take away anything else that others have. Do you understand?"

"Yes, I understand, but you could have told me before the last day of school. I need to figure out how to tell Isabelle. And I won't be able to see Nathan again. It's unfair. And I don't understand why you lied to me, Maminou. We always tell each other everything. I've never lied to you. That was our agreement—no lies, no secrets."

"I know, my little Sylvestre, and I apologize. Who is Nathan, my dear?"

"Nobody," I lied. "Bye, I have to go tell my best friend that we only have two weeks to see each other and then we'll never see each other again. I hate you." And with that, I hung up the phone.

I sat for a moment crying before heading to Isabelle's house. Knowing my grandmother well, I'm sure she's crying right now, and it pains me because I love her deeply. Maminou is also like a mother to me. Having not had a mother, she filled that role in a way. She taught me womanly things, so to speak. Like when I got my period, I was so scared when I woke up in the morning that I ran to her house without telling my father. She reassured me, telling me I was now a woman. That from now on, I could have children. That my body would produce eggs to have babies.

She explained everything to me calmly, talking to me as an adult, not a child. You might wonder why I don't have a mom. Well, she left us one morning when I was very young. I'm not quite sure why. I don't remember if Dad ever told me, and she never came back. I was little, but my father filled the role of both parents so well that I never felt the lack, especially with Maminou and Grandpa around. Maminou, in particular, made sure I didn't miss Stella too much. Oh, I don't call her 'mom.' I don't have a mother, so I'm standing in front of Isabelle's house, not knowing how to break the news to her.

I love this stone field house with its large front display window, the dormers up top, the grand wooden door, and the beautiful flowers that her mom and Isabelle planted together long ago. I'm going to miss this house terribly. Tears welled up in my eyes just as Isabelle opened the door.

"Hey, your grandmother called to tell me you were coming over and that you had something difficult to tell me." She noticed I was crying as she finished speaking. "What's wrong? Has something happened to your dad or your grandfather? Why are you crying? Come on, let's go to my room." She took me by the neck and, without speaking to her mother, led me to her room and closed the door behind us.

This room, where we grew up together, I would miss dearly. Isabelle and I have known each other forever. How do I tell her that we will be apart from now on? That we would no longer have projects together, that from today onwards, we would no longer be daily confidants? I cried uncontrollably. Isabelle held me in her arms, rocking me on her bed, allowing me to cry so that I could eventually explain everything to her. After several minutes, which felt like hours, I managed to tell her what was happening. I continued to cry throughout.

"We're moving," I said, grabbing a tissue to wipe my nose.

"...? Moving??? What do you mean?"

"My dad has decided that we need to move. And Maminou and Grandpa are going to live with us in the same house."

"What?" Isabelle was so surprised that she jumped out of bed. "I don't understand. Why? Are they sick?"

"No, I don't think so. They would have told me."

"Then why suddenly do they need to go live with you?"

"I don't know, and I didn't want to talk to my dad. I was so angry yesterday after coming back from school that I fell asleep in my bed, exhausted from crying. I woke up this morning at 4:00 a.m., still dressed, lying at the wrong end of my bed. I went downstairs to eat because I was hungry, he was sleeping in the living room. He must have been waiting for me there, thinking I'd come back for dinner, but I fell asleep. Then I took a hot shower to think, and I didn't feel like talking to him, so I left quietly and went to sit in the park. I had brought Nathan's letter, which I hadn't read. And now I'm here."

"And Nathan's letter?" Isabelle asked, curious.

"It's lovely. He wants us to meet during the summer, go to the movies, take walks, and all..." I started to cry again. Isabelle took me in her arms.

"Don't cry. You'll be able to see him even if you move."

"No, it will be too far." Isabelle looked at me with wide eyes.

"How far exactly?"

"I don't know, but my father told me it's a few hours from here. A few hours means it's not doable by bike. Nathan wanted to talk to me all year, but he was busy with school and hockey, and now that we can see each other, I'm moving." I cried even more now. Isabelle remained silent.

"You don't have to move that far away. Let's go and see your father and ask him the whole truth. Together, he will have no choice but to tell us everything. Wipe your eyes, and let's go."

"Okay, you will remain my best friend no matter the distance between us. And nothing will stop me from coming to see you. It's a good thing we can see each other every day through our tablets. We can also call each other every day. We still have at least two weeks to enjoy our fireplace and see each other. And the journey can probably be made by bus too."

"What? Two weeks? You didn't tell me you were moving in two weeks!"

"I forgot. Yes, we're moving in two weeks. That's why all the cardboard boxes around the house were about. I thought Dad was cleaning the attic, but we're moving in two weeks. He said he didn't want to tell me earlier so I could have a 'normal' last year of high school like all the other students."

"A normal year? What does that even mean?" Isabelle asked as she walked towards my house.

"That's what I asked him. I found it strange, too. He said he didn't want me to be preoccupied with the move and wanted me to fully enjoy my last year of high school. He said that it was an important and decisive year for me." We stopped at the end of my yard, facing each other, and looked into each other's eyes.

"All this, it's bizarre. I feel like he's hiding something. But since you didn't get a chance to talk with your dad yesterday, we'll ask our questions today. I want to know why I'm losing my best friend and your father better have a good reason." Isabelle was agitated and ready to confront my father.

"I'll let you ask him your questions; I think I'll just burst into tears," I said, with tears overflowing from my eyes.

In each other's arms, we moved toward the front door of my house. I opened the door and took a deep breath. My father was waiting in the kitchen with three glasses of iced tea. I looked at him, surprised, pointing at the three glasses on the table.

"Your grandmother called me, Isabelle, when you left. She warned me that, metaphorically speaking, you were coming fully prepared for battle. I'm ready to answer all your questions. Go ahead!" Louis was calm.

We sat down and sipped on that homemade iced tea—the best. At least I had ants in my pants, a dry throat, and clammy hands. I glanced at Isabelle, signaling that it was her turn to speak. Slightly taller than me, Isabelle had a somewhat rebellious or fierce appearance to some. She had the demeanor of a fighter. A bit unruly, yes, but the best friend one could have. She looked at me with her large, light green eyes, pushed back her very light blond hair, and took a deep breath.

"You're going to tell us the whole truth and nothing but the truth. The why and how, the where and when. And no lies allowed," Isabelle said with an incredible calmness and seriousness I had never seen in her before.

"Absolutely, no problem. I completely agree with that. So, where should I begin?"

"Start by telling us why," Isabelle suggested.

"Because I'm running out of space here for my work. I need a bigger place."

"And where exactly are you moving to?"

"A bit far, I admit. It's an eight-hour drive from here."

"What? Have you lost your mind? It's an eight-hour drive. Wasn't there any place closer suitable for your needs? Why so far away?" I nearly shouted at him.

"You're going to love our new house. It's very big, with a forest surrounding it. Grandma and Grandpa will be living with us."

"We're going to live in the forest? Come on, seriously. I won't like that! I'll be far from everyone I love. Why in the woods? I don't understand."

"Because I need more space to make swords."

"You're an architect, Dad, not a sword maker. What do you call a sword maker?"

"An armorer," my father replied calmly.

"An armorer! Come on, Dad, that's not a thing; you're making it up."

"You're lying, I can feel it!" said Isabelle, looking him straight in the eye.

"No, I'm not lying. I need more space, both for my weapons and my drafting tables. And this house, in a way, belongs to our family lineage. Thanks to Grandma, we inherited it, in a sense."

"I don't understand, and you seem to be lying to me, Dad. Why have I never heard of this family with a huge house in the woods before? You're hiding something from me."

"Firstly, it's not in the woods. There's a forest behind and around it. And you'll understand when you see it."

"No, because I won't go with you."

"And where will you go, my dear?"

"To my place," Isabelle replied quickly. "I'm sure my parents will want to take Lilou with us."

"That's out of the question. You're coming with me."

"Why? Why can't I stay here and go to school with Isabelle? Speaking of school, what school would I go to? A school where I learn to chop down trees or make my own pencils from old branches?" And at that moment, my grandparents entered the house.

"No, Lilou, you're not going to learn to make your own pencils, silly. But you're going to love the college there. It's really beautiful and not far from the house."

"A college?" Isabelle repeated.

"Yes, college, because it's private."

"I don't want to go to a private school; I want to attend a regular one. I want to go to school with Isabelle. I don't want to be separated from Isabelle. We're going to become nurses together."

"Listen, my dear, I'm truly sorry, but we have to go. I need this space, and I'm sure you'll love it there. We're moving in two weeks. Until then, you can be together here every day, have bonfires every night, and sleep outside if you want. I have very warm sleeping bags. I can even set up a shelter for you in case it rains. But this is where the discussion ends. You need to start packing, and Isabelle is welcome to help. Grandma and Grandpa came to help me finish packing everything. Do what you want; we're leaving in two weeks," my father said firmly, standing up, and he left the room, indicating the discussion was over. Grandma didn't dare look at me anymore. She turned around and left for another room.

During the two weeks that followed, Isabelle and I had fires every evening and sometimes even in the afternoon. We ate marshmallows, grilled sausages on the fire, and slept under the stars many nights—every night, in fact. We took all our meals outside. Even Isabelle's parents, who understood very well what we were going through, would bring us meals so we could spend as much time together as possible. On rainy nights, we slept in my room. Dad would even bring us extra wood on other nights so we wouldn't get too cold. I didn't speak to him the first week nor to my grandparents either. They didn't speak to me either. I think they understood that I needed that time and didn't want to lose a single minute with Isabelle. Isabelle, my best friend, I was going to miss her so much. How would I manage without her? She was the one who defended me at school when people were mean to me or when a teacher scolded me. She would immediately stand up for me. It was as if she felt obliged to protect me all the time.

During the first week, I called Nathan and arranged to talk with him at the park. Isabelle didn't come with me, even though she didn't want me to go alone. I told her that this was something I had to do by myself. Then I explained to Nathan that we were moving in a week because of my father's job. No, I didn't know until today, and I was sad he hadn't talked to me sooner. I genuinely hoped we could remain friends and that we could still write to each other or talk on FaceTime. And how much I would have liked to be his girlfriend.

"I wish you could have been my girlfriend, too. I regret listening to my mother so much now and never writing to or talking to you at school. However, I'm shy, and Isabelle is quite intimidating. It's not an excuse, but she's scary, you know? May I kiss you? I wish you could have been my first kiss."

"Yes, you can kiss me. I really wish we had talked before today." He came closer to me, took my face in his hands, and kissed me. It was the first time a boy had kissed me. It was the first time anyone had kissed me, at least in that way. I don't like girls in that way. I don't know why I specified a boy, I wouldn't want to kiss a girl. Anyway, it was gentle, warm, and moist. I loved it. Our kiss lasted for a while, and our breathing grew a bit faster. We stayed there for a good while, pressed against each other, sitting at the base of a tree. We talked about many things. He couldn't understand why my father hadn't told me earlier, and I told him I didn't understand either.

"I'm happy you were my first kiss. We'll write to each other, and if I ever play in your area, maybe we can arrange to see each other. You could come to watch me play. Where are you moving to, actually?"

"I don't even know what it's called, I didn't ask, but I know it's an eight-hour drive from here."

"Eight hours? Wow, that's really far. But I travel far to play. Sometimes, we have to stay overnight after a match because it's too far."

"Maybe we can meet again then. You have my number. Call me if you ever come my way. I'll ask my dad the name of the town. I'll write it down for you tonight, and we can meet up, and I'll come and cheer you on."

"I really hope we can meet again. I regret even more now that I didn't talk to you from the first day I saw you. In our first math class, I saw you walking in with your long wheat-colored hair. Wow, I had such a hard time concentrating. All year, I struggled to focus in that class."

"Next time you want to talk to someone, don't wait. Just do it right away, okay?"

"Yes. I'll try to get over my shyness," he said as he kissed me again. First kiss. Wow.

At the end of the first week, I asked my dad to throw a small party to say goodbye to all my friends whom I never dreamed I'd see again. I knew I would see Isabelle again. I couldn't bear the thought of never seeing her again, even if I didn't have other friends. There were people at school with whom I got along well and whom I wanted to bid farewell, like Nathan. So, I wanted to have a small outdoor party with a fire in the evening to tell them I was leaving and we wouldn't see each other again. I wanted to wish them luck in their new schools, which I wouldn't know. I wanted to see Nathan one last time, see friendly faces, and share a laugh before facing the reality that I would be alone there. Of course, my dad agreed. The party was wonderful. Everyone agreed to come.

Many even brought their tents to stay up later. Some ended up sleeping on lounge chairs. A few three-person tents even squeezed into five, tightly packed. I don't know how they managed to sleep all crammed together like that. Some people brought sausages and marshmallows to roast over the fire. Some brought drinks, chips, and candies. I was very surprised and pleased; I found it very kind, even though I hadn't asked for anything.

Nathan arrived with a keen desire to see me again before my departure. We stayed glued together all evening, sharing several more kisses. There were more girls, but to my surprise, quite a few boys also showed up. I'm not sure how many of us there were, but certainly more than twenty. Some will pursue advanced sciences, others arts. One girl is heading to a private school for music, and I'm genuinely happy for her; she plays the piano so beautifully. As for me, I don't understand music at all. I love it, but I can only listen to it. Nathan and I remained inseparable throughout the evening, and he stayed over.

We slept side by side on a lounge chair, holding hands in an utterly romantic sleeping bag. The music, the fire, the snacks, and my friends' laughter lifted my spirits. My grandparents prepared an amazing breakfast for everyone: toast made over an outdoor fire, eggs, pancakes, and orange juice. Nearly everyone left at the same time. Saying goodbye was hard. Some of my friends left me their contact information, Instagram, or other platforms to stay in touch. It's a way to keep updating each other in our new schools and facing new challenges. Isabelle stayed with me, though. There was no way we were wasting a single minute of the time we could spend together.

I only have three days left. I haven't even started packing yet. It's as if I'm hoping my dad will change his mind at the last minute, or that I'll wake up and realize it was all just a nightmare. But now I need to hurry if I don't want my father barging into my room and haphazardly throwing things into boxes just to finish it quickly because we're out of time. After breakfast, Isabelle will come to help. We'll blast music, listening to the sweet sounds of BTS or the Jonas Brothers—Kevin is my favorite. Everything needs to be finished by tomorrow. Isabelle will spend the penultimate night here with me. I can't imagine being without her. What will I do without my best friend to talk with, to discuss boys, or anything else? I can't bear to think about it. I can't envision my life without her. When she arrived, after I had put my cereal bowl in the sink and heard her laughing and saying hello, my heart burst, and I broke down in tears. I hugged Isabelle and told her how much I was going to miss her.

"Let's go upstairs," she said, looking at my father darkly.

The music and Isabelle's laughter made me feel better and helped me pack. I set a lot of things aside: clothes that no longer fit, clothes I didn't like anymore, and clothes that were too old. I made three piles: to keep, to donate, or to throw away. For donations, there was more than one box. I think I had never really cleaned out my wardrobe before. I still had old stuffed animals from childhood and the pink roller skates with glitter that I glued with Grandma. It felt good, even though I was not too fond of the reason why. I opened my door and asked my Grandpa to come and see me for a moment.

"What is it, my dear?"

"Grandpa, can you please help me take these boxes to the donation center?"

"Yes, of course. Are you sure there's nothing in these boxes you want to keep?"

"Absolutely, they're all things that are too small, that I don't like anymore, or from when I was very little."

"Alright, let's take them down and get them to the center-right away so we don't mix up the boxes."

The next day, the last day before the big move, was mostly quiet. A day for checking, for last-minute packing to prepare for the long journey.

"Which one of these magazines do you want to keep with you for the trip?" Isabelle asked me.

"Just keep three, I should be good with those. I haven't read them yet, so choose at random."

"And do you want me to set up your music playlist on your phone for the trip?"

"Yes, you can do that. I'll let you choose, so I'll be surprised. I'm going to empty my bathroom." Yes, I had a bathroom to myself in my room with a shower, a toilet, and a large mirror. I hope I'll still have my bathroom in this new damn house that I'm sure I'll hate, especially since there will be two more of us now. KNOCK, KNOCK, KNOCK. Someone was knocking at my bedroom door.

"Yes, come in."

"Hey girls, I've brought you your dinner. I thought you might like to be here alone, have some peace and quiet, and just eat among yourselves, so I got you a pizza just the way you like it, half veggie and half all-dressed, and two cold iced teas."

"Thanks, Dad, that's a great idea."

"Thank you so much, Louis," said Isabelle.

"Enjoy your meal."

The Big Meetings

Waking up this morning in my bed, I looked around at my room's pale pink and turquoise walls for the last time. It no longer resembled its former self, with boxes and suitcases strewn all over. All my frames were removed. The photos of my friends and I were no longer on the bulletin board, which now lay on the floor wrapped in a large beach towel to protect it from potential damage during the move. It was a project I crafted with my dad years ago, a plastic art project for school. I got an A, thankfully, due to my dad's help. Without him, I probably would have ended up with a C, or maybe even a C-. I'm not good at visual arts, not in drawing, painting, or anything creative, really. My father and I are moving.

My name is Lilou. To be honest, my real name is Liliane, but I've never liked that name. Since I was little, I've asked people to call me Lilou, and my real name, Liliane, has since been forgotten. My father says we're moving because of his job. He's an architect and an armorer. Don't ask me why armorer—all I know is he has a passion for ancient weapons like swords and crossbows. He enjoys carving the handles from a sacred tree branch, such as the Lapacho.

The Lapacho is a magnificent tree with trumpet-shaped pink flowers, primarily found on the firm lands of the Amazon rainforest's tropical zones and in South America's temperate areas. Its height ranges from 20 to 50 meters or 65 to 164 feet. It's tall and the only tree in that region entirely immune to infections from the numerous fungi in these humid areas. Its color varies from white to very dark purple, passing through all shades of pink. The heartwood, the hard part in the center of the tree, is traditionally used by the Indigenous people to make bows. The sapwood, the layer between the bark and the heart of the tree, is also used. The circulating sap is used to fight various infections. Its therapeutic and nutritional properties have been used since time immemorial to cure and prevent the spread of numerous infections and diseases.

So, the leftover bark and the unused ends of my father's bow carvings go to Grand-Mi. She makes antibiotics and brews teas loaded with potassium, calcium, and iron, which possess great healing powers and strengthen the immune system. But let's move on. That's not super interesting! What really matters to me right now are my friends, whom I'm leaving today, and my life here, which I quite adore. To be more precise, very much so. But Dad insists that we absolutely have to move there to that remote spot in the woods.

Hooray!

Dad also makes sheaths to slip the blades into, which he forges. So he says that where we're moving, he'll have more space, with a large outdoor hearth to melt and forge the metals for the blades. The place should also inspire him to design new houses, given that he is primarily an architect. I'm not sure about that, but I have no say since parents always decide without asking us for our opinion first!

So here we are, it's six o'clock in the morning, and the moving trucks will be here at 10. Yes, it's early, especially for a teenager. But I still have lots of things to pack into boxes and my last suitcase to close.

We kept all the bedding from the bathroom and the dishes for the last week because we didn't eat from styrofoam plates like Granny during that previous week. Oh, definitely not! My father says it's bad for the environment. So, we had to pack up everything we had used in the previous week. I stripped the bed sheets, a few books, and my mom's personal belongings. They're already in boxes but still in the attic, and Dad refuses to remove them. He's holding onto the hope that she'll return, but not me. Mom left one fine morning before dawn when I was five years old. I don't remember much about her. I have pictures, and I know I look a lot like her, just like my grandmother and great-grandmother. Strange, but true. We all have dark green eyes with orange rays inside. It makes it look like there's a sun in the eye. Long, sun-bleached hair, which grows back very quickly when cut. I never understood why. I have a small, delicate nose with an incredible sense of smell.

One morning, not too long ago, when I woke up, I sensed the lilacs from our third neighbor blooming. I can smell scents from miles away. Grandma says we have the same hands, even though hers are old and wrinkled, they are identical. My grandparents are coming to live with us. That's going to be strange. Dad says the house is big enough. We might not even see each other for days because it's so large. You shouldn't always believe what he says. He's always been one for exaggeration.

From my room, I could smell the freshly ground coffee and the bacon and eggs that Dad was making for breakfast. Mmm, yummy! Someone knocked on my door.

"Come in."

"Hello, my dear, are you coming to have breakfast with us?" asked my grandfather Alfred.

"Grandpa, what are you doing here so early this morning?"

"We've come to eat with you and help pack the remaining things before the big move. We've been ready for ages, you know, Adèle."

"Yes, I know, Grandma. I'm sure you've been eating off of styrofoam plates for at least a week."

"No, two weeks. Come on, the coffee is hot, and the bacon is just how you like it, crispy. I made it myself."

"Mmm, my mouth is watering already. I'll get dressed and be right down."

My grandfather is a very handsome man. Even today, despite his age, women turn around to look at him as he passes. He has that certain something that attracts all women. I can't quite put my finger on it. Is it in his gaze, his smile, or perhaps his strong, proud demeanor? He keeps fit and has a very handsome figure for a grandpa. He runs every morning before breakfast and still goes to the gym. My grandma is also very beautiful. My grandparents really don't look their age. They seem at least ten years younger, maybe even more.

It's quite peculiar when I look at my friends' grandparents. They truly seem to be 60 years old or older. I hope to be like them. Of course, I need to run every day and eat less cake... That's the tough part.

While savoring our breakfast, we discussed the journey. It will take eight hours to reach our destination. We will make only one stop. We can't stop too often with the moving trucks. Everything must be planned before departure. Do not drink too much to avoid the need for bathroom breaks. We brought music, headphones, snacks, magazines, and sunglasses, even if the day looked rainy and fresh. Maminou, I sometimes call my grandmother that because she is both a mother and grandmother to me, made us chicken-mayonnaise sandwiches with basil, crustless, just how I like them. With a thermos of homemade lemonade and two-colored chocolate chip cookies, Dad's favorites. They are so good; they're everyone's favorite.

After breakfast, the men emptied the attic, and we women gathered and finished packing up everything that was left. We emptied the fridge into an electric cooler. I took out the last trash bags and went to the roadside to clean the fridge for the trip. After placing the most fragile items in the two cars, like mirrors, plants, and some of Dad's cherished trinkets, Maminou and I did one last tour of the house to make sure nothing was left behind. We checked all the cabinets and closets and returned to the attic to ensure the men hadn't forgotten anything.

I was gazing out at the yard from my second-floor bedroom window. I'll never see this scenery again. I love our backyard, with the fieldstone fireplace that my friend Isabelle and I built. We carried three or four stones at a time in my dad's wheelbarrow to build our future bonfire for roasting marshmallows on girls' nights. We spent several nights under the stars, snug in our sleeping bags on a lounge chair, shivering cold as the fire died down. But I'd sleep there again in a heartbeat to stay here. The spooky stories Grandpa used to tell Isabelle and me. The fits of laughter we had in this yard. I treasure those memories dearly. I'm going to miss my life here. I wiped away my tears with my T-shirt sleeve.

"Lilou, can you come here? There's someone outside for you," called my father from the bottom of the stairs.

"Go ahead, my little wild mallow, I'll finish up," my grandmother told me.

As I approached the door, I recognized the scent of Isabelle's perfume before even seeing her. She smells of wild berries. Isabelle's eyes were reddened, and she held a gift in the hollow of her hands. Seeing my best friend with such a sad look, I couldn't help but burst into tears and throw myself into her arms.

"I will miss you so much, Lilou. What am I going to do without you every day? You're like my family; I feel more at home here than in my own house."

"I know. You're like our family to my father and me, too. You are the sister I never had, and my father has always considered you as his second daughter. We're going to miss you too." Lilou let Isabelle inside; she was soaked from the rainy day.

"I brought you a gift. It's something that belonged to my father. My biological father, and I absolutely want you to have it with you at all times." Lilou carefully took the package wrapped in pink paper, her favorite color. She opened it gently.

"Oh my God, it's your father's compass that you've always worn around your neck. I can't accept this; it's your lucky charm."

"Yes, I want you to have it. I want you to be able to find your way back at all times, no matter where you are in the world. You will be in the north, and I will be in the south. We will always be on the same line, and I will feel like I am with you all the time."

"Thank you, Isabelle. I will only take it off to go in the shower. I'm going to miss you so much." Her father arrived behind them and embraced both girls.

"You will really be missed a lot, Isabelle, but I have a surprise for both of you." They turned to look at Louis with a look of surprise.

"I asked your parents if you could come and spend the summer holidays with us, and... they accepted. You will take the train at the beginning of July, and a bus will take you home."

We were so excited about the good news that we started dancing and shouting like two children at Christmas, seeing tons of gifts under the tree on the morning of the 25th.

"You will also have to thank Adèle and Alfred. They worked very hard to convince your parents that they will be your guardians."

We ran off and jumped into their arms, thanking them a thousand times.

"You will be together in about two weeks. We thought that Lilou would like to have her best friend with her for her birthday in August. And that maybe, it will be easier for the two of you to continue your new challenge. And your parents also agreed to let you come and spend all the great holidays with us. So, School Break Week, Easter holidays, Christmas, and so on."

"You are the best grandparents in the world!" I said to my grandparents.

"You are mine too since I don't have any others anyway!" says Isabelle, crazy with joy.

"But you have always been a member of our family, Isabelle," replied Maminou in a somewhat strange tone to the girls' ears. But, too happy, they did not pay too much attention to the remark.

The road was long, VERY long. I felt like I was changing countries so much. The scenery changed as we left our hometown. I only saw trees and trees and still more trees. I have already gone through the music directory on my iPod twice. I looked at all the magazines I brought in my bag, and I was hungry like a wolf. We had already eaten all of Grandma's chicken sandwiches without crust and the cookies too.

The moving trucks arrived at ten o'clock, but it took three hours to empty my grandparents' house and ours into the two trucks. The two trucks were so lengthy that I doubted they could navigate the street corners. I was amazed at how effortlessly those men could maneuver such elongated vehicles anywhere. We departed at 1:00 PM; the journey should take around eight hours, plus a stop of about an hour to stretch our legs and eat at supper time. We should arrive around ten in the evening, provided everything goes well with just one stop. It's now 6:00 PM.

"Ah, there's the next stop in 3 km. We'll halt to eat, stretch a bit, and refuel the cars and trucks," Louis announced, spotting the road sign.

"At last, I'm starving and can't stand sitting anymore. It feels like there are ants in my legs, and my buttocks are completely numb," I replied.

The rest of the trip after that brief stop of an hour and a half, refueling both trucks, the two cars, and having dinner, took longer than expected. So, the last remaining kilometers seemed even longer. Even though my father and I were singing at the top of our lungs and telling jokes to pass the time, playing the game of who sees a car of a certain color first, who spots a bird first, and who sees a boat first, I couldn't take it anymore. There are even songs in my music playlist that I won't be able to listen to anymore. Never again.

"Ah, Dad, I can't take it anymore. How much longer do we have approximately?"

"I believe we are close now, according to the GPS. I'll call Mr. Henry to ask him to turn on the lights I had installed along the driveway to see better where we're going," my father said.

"Who is Mr. Henry, Dad?"

"He's our handyman. Gardener, plumber, cook, whatever you need. He does it all."

"And does he live with us?"

"No, he has his own home at the end of the property. He was here before with the previous owners, and I agreed to keep him on. I thought he would be very useful, and besides, he asks for almost nothing."

"Why did the previous owners want to sell?"

"They said the forest was haunted and preferred the big city." I can't tell her the real reason why they gave us their place. She needs to be close to the forest and near the school, too, Louis said to himself.

"What?! You bought a house next to a haunted forest? That's not right. And you're telling me this now when we're almost there?"

"I didn't believe them. Let's see, Lilou, those things don't exist."

"How do you know? Did you check?"

"No, but the price and the location were really appealing to me, and I don't believe in ghosts."

Dad called Mr. Henry and asked him to turn on the lights because we were almost there.

"Thank you, Mr. Henry, you are really kind... Me too, am very eager to introduce everyone to you, see you soon."

He ended the call with a smile on his face. It always amuses me to see people talking on the phone with both hands on the steering wheel. Or encountering someone at the supermarket with both hands on the shopping cart, and they seem to be talking to themselves. However, they're speaking into their little earpiece. Technology moves fast.

"What's making you smile so much?"

"He is nice, he had already turned them all on. He wanted us to spot the house from the road. Look at the top of the mountain, that's our house." He pointed out a luminous dwelling atop a mountain. But it was so far and high that it was hard to determine what the house looked like. From here, it looked like a birdhouse with interior lights. I took a photo with my cellphone. I'll send it to Isabelle later."

"Dad, will we have Wi-Fi? Please say yes because I would go crazy without it."

"Yes, darling, we have Wi-Fi. It was installed a few weeks ago, and I'll need it for work, too. Don't worry, you'll be able to, how do you say, 'chat?' With your friends."

"Yes, Dad, 'chat.' You're so funny. It's just for quick communication with Isabelle. I don't have anyone else to write to anyway." Even though he was often on my mind, I didn't want to talk to him about Nathan. I sent him the details of our new house, just in case he would come by this remote place."

"Yes, you'll be able to write to her, my dear, once we arrive."

Upon reaching our house's driveway, I was stunned, by a massive gate. Large metal doors guarded the entrance like some Hollywood star's mansion. The design featured a gigantic tree when both doors closed together. The driveway was lined with trees, illuminated by ground lights all along the path—magnificent willows centuries old. The approach to the house seemed endless. I took numerous photos.

"Wow, Dad, have you seen the size of the house? It looks like several houses fused together. And all these lights."

"Now you understand why I said we might even have trouble running into the grandparents, given its vast size."

"Yes, I get it now. It's amazing; I can't wait for Isabelle to see this. Can I choose my room?"

"Yes, but I already know which one you're going to pick."

"Oh really? Why, and which one is it?"

"If I tell you, I'll influence your choice. I'll let you know afterward."

"Okay, but no cheating then."

"I promise," Dad made the sign of the cross over his heart. "Cross my heart and hope to die, stick a needle in my eye if I lie!"

I saw an old, bent man coming out of the house.

"Is that Mr. Henry?" I asked my father with a look of disbelief.

"Yes, you'll see, he's really kind. Did I tell you that Mr. Henry was born here in this house?"

"No, but you mentioned he's a jack-of-all-trades. Dad, he can hardly do anything now. Didn't you see how old he is? He has trouble getting around. But is this his family's house?"

"No, he worked here all his life. His mother was also a housemaid in the past. They've always lived here in the servants' quarters at the back of the yard. And he still accomplishes a lot; you'll be surprised."

"Wow, he must know some incredible stories about this house then."

"Yes, probably," my father replied, parking the car further away to make room for the trucks.

My father and I got out of the car to meet him with my grandparents.

"Welcome to all of you, it's extremely nice to see you again finally, Mr. Louis." Henry fixed his gaze on Lilou, and a silence seemed to last an eternity. "Miss, you will love this house. You will feel right at home. I could show you hiding places I only know in this mansion," he winked.

"I'd like that, Mr. Henry," I responded, feeling a bit uneasy. "That way, I can hide from Dad."

"Hey! Don't start ganging up on me, you two."

"But of course not, Mr. Louis, I would never do such a thing," Mr. Henry replied, giving me another knowing wink. "Come, let me show you around your new residence. Welcome to His Majesty's abode." He also greeted my grandparents, whom my father introduced before we entered the vast house.

Everyone was captivated by the size of the house. Mr. Henry shared that during the construction, all the trees that were cut down to make space, not just for the house but also for the stables at the back, which, regrettably, stand abandoned today, were repurposed within the house. The floors, the steps, the frame of the main fireplace in the living room, and many doors were all crafted from these trees. The remaining wood, too small or too old to be reused, was chopped for firewood. However, local artisans made sure to salvage as many of these sacred trees as possible, like the tree-shaped coat stand at the entrance and several candelabras and pieces of furniture.

"Why do you call them sacred trees?" I inquired.

"It's because..." Mr. Henry turned towards Louis with a look seeking assistance. "It's because these trees were over three hundred years old. And the owners wanted, in a way, to thank them for providing a home." Louis thought to himself that Mr. Henry had handled that well.

"Ah, I see. Can I go upstairs and choose my room?"

"With pleasure. I advise you to visit them all before making your decision."

"Why is that?"

"Because I am certain of the one you will choose, but at least you will have seen them all before," Mr. Henry confidently replied.

"Why? What's so special about this room that I am supposed to choose? Dad, do you think it's the same one that you said I would pick?"

"I don't know, my dear, but visit them all, and we'll see after. You'll find that each one has its own little something special."

I climbed the numerous steps to reach the second floor, taking them two at a time, excited to discover my new room. I started with the first on the right of the stairs, as my father and Mr. Henry had suggested. Large, with a double wardrobe, a private bathroom, and two windows overlooking the forest on the side of the house. No, this room didn't speak to me. I moved on to the second bedroom. Slightly smaller, it featured a large window and a mini walk-in closet. I went from room to room until I reached the last one at the end of the corridor, on the far side of the house to the right. There were six rooms in total on this floor, three on each side of the hallway. Opening the door, a sense of belonging overwhelmed me. There were four massive windows overlooking the forest. It seemed there were no corners, with the windows in pairs on the end walls, meeting in such a way that the view was absolutely extraordinary. It felt like being in the middle of the forest or as if the forest was in the room.

"A fireplace made of large stones, which I was sure had been gathered from outside, one by one, just like the fireplace I had built with Isabelle. A private bathroom in turquoise, oddly one of my favorite colors. A closet large enough to fit a cot and a fabulous barn wood floor. I lay down on the floor and took a deep breath. A peculiar sensation filled my body. I truly felt as if the floor was embracing me. Looking out the window, with all the lights on, I could see birds strolling and butterflies flitting about. Are the animals awake at night?! What are they doing up at this hour?

"And have you chosen your room, my little wildflower?" I got up and hugged my grandmother.

"Yes, and you know what? I felt like it was the room that chose me. It's as if this room was made for me. Look at the bathroom. It's my favorite color."

"Wow, it's wonderful. This room and the view outside are absolutely magnificent. I'm jealous. I can't wait to see the sun streaming in here during the day."

"You and grandfather should have it. You two would be so comfortable here with the fireplace in winter."

"No, no, it's yours. We'll sleep downstairs. The stairs are starting to become a challenge for us, and it will only get worse."

"Okay, agreed, then let's go see yours, Grandma."

No one slept much that night. Surprisingly, we arrived at eleven o'clock, and by 2 a.m., all the trucks and cars were emptied. It took less time to unload everything than to load. We were all eager to sleep, I believe. We all slept on a piece of mattress on the floor, wrapped in a blanket. I didn't even take the time to undress. I had only removed my shoes. The truckers slept on the sofas in the living room. Louis couldn't let them leave before getting a night's sleep. The risk of a road accident was too high. Oddly, the men did not refuse. At 6 a.m., I was awakened by the sun penetrating through the many windows of my room. Birds and butterflies perched on the ledge of my window as if welcoming me. What better way to start the day than with a nice hot shower and clean clothes, especially with so little sleep? But honestly, I felt in great shape. I think it was the excitement.

I went down the grand staircase, made of old planks from the old stable renovated entirely years ago. Mr. Henry explained yesterday if I understood correctly, but unfortunately, it is now abandoned due to a lack of staff. There used to be great breeds of competition horses here. But after the wars, the owners lost many of their employees and couldn't keep the stables active. So they sold all their horses and let the stables become what they are today. An old building was abandoned at the back of the property. I wanted to prepare coffee and some scrambled eggs for everyone.

Roughly halfway to my destination, I caught the delightful aroma of coffee and bacon eggs. Mr. Henry was in the kitchen, having prepared everything already. The table was set, with a place for each one of us. Fruits, cereals, freshly squeezed orange juice, and a pint of milk were all laid out on the table.

"Wow, Mr. Henry, you went out of your way for us this morning!"

"Not at all, I always prepare breakfast. I always wake up very early, and it's the day's most important meal."

"I have a feeling I'm going to like you a lot, Mr. Henry, because breakfast is my favorite meal, and I adore bacon and eggs."

"I'm very pleased to hear that. Go ahead and eat. You'll need plenty of energy today."

"Why?"

Mr. Henry hesitated. "Because you have many boxes to unpack today, a lot of furniture to arrange, and the forest to explore," he replied, taking wheat muffins out of the oven.

"Ah yes, I'm looking forward to walking there. How do you avoid getting lost? It's so vast?"

"Don't worry, it's impossible for you to get lost, dear Lilou. The forest is your home," Mr. Henry said, turning away. Oops! What had he just said... He closed his eyes for a moment, hoping she hadn't understood too much and wouldn't ask any questions.

I found him really strange, but I couldn't say anything because everyone arrived at the same moment to have breakfast and drink that wonderfully smelling coffee. The meal was greatly enjoyed. It was a meal just the way I liked it, filled with much discussion, many questions often unanswered, and a variety of opinions. Mr. Henry joined in the discussions and seemed happy. Strangely, he looked younger than last night upon our arrival. Having people around him seemed to do him the greatest good. I believe he had been alone for too long, radiating happiness. He looked up at me, gave me his most beautiful smile, and winked. Finally, life was going to resume here, he thought. He felt the earth trembling with joy. The truck drivers appreciated the breakfast before they left.

"Tell me, is it true that the forest is haunted, Mr. Henry?"

"What? No. The forest isn't haunted, but it is inhabited by many animals."

"What kind?"

"Squirrels, various types of birds, skunks, raccoons, deer, foxes, and many more. But no animal poses a danger to us. No bears or wolves. There are wolves in the area, but they are really farther away. They have never come here."

"All right. I'm truly relieved."

After lunch, the truck drivers set off again, thanking my father for allowing them to sleep over instead of hitting the road again and for sharing the morning meal with them.

After several hours of tidying up, Adèle entered my room with a tray laden with grapes, cheese, and crustless chicken sandwiches, accompanied by two large glasses of ice-cold milk.

"Shall we have a little snack, just us girls?"

"Yes, I'm really very hungry Maminou, and a little break would be most welcome."

We chatted while savoring our dinner, seated on the floor on a very comfortable rug. It had been there upon our arrival, rolled up in the closet. Facing the windows, we looked outside at the splendid view of the forest. With such large windows nearly reaching the floor, it truly felt like sitting outside. A swallow landed on the ledge of the open window and seemed to look at me.

"Wow, a swallow, Grand-mi. Look, it seems like it's watching me."

"That's true, it's quite odd, isn't it?" The bird flew away, singing. They looked at each other in silence. Butterflies, dragonflies, and several birds came near the window as if to greet them.

"Do you think they are happy or displeased that we're here? I've never seen animals come up to a window like this before."

"I believe they are very happy that we're finally here to feed them! I've brought all my feeders, let's go fill them outside. It would be like telling them, 'Welcome to our home."

"Great Idea, grand-MI, and It's such beautIful weather, we should definitely enjoy it a bit."

"But first, I have a little surprise for you. I was waiting for the right moment to give it to you, and I think now is the perfect time." She pulled out a large envelope from behind her back, wearing a big smile.

"What is it, Maminou?"

"If I tell you before you open it, it won't be a surprise anymore, so do you want me to tell you what's inside, or do you want to discover it yourself?" she asked me, hand resting on the envelope.

"By myself." I opened the envelope, which was filled with photos. She took pictures of Isabelle and me on the last day of school. During our walk home, here are photos of us from a few weeks ago. "How did you manage to take these pictures? We didn't see you."

"That was the point. These are memories, I didn't want them to be staged. I wanted real memories. Keep looking at the other pictures."

There were photos from the few days Isabelle and I spent by the fire. There were beautiful photos of the two of us. Pictures from the party I threw before leaving. Lovely images with my friends, with laughter and funny faces. Photos with Isabelle, me, and our girlfriends. And three beautiful photos of Nathan and me. One where we are talking while looking into each other's eyes. Another where we are close and sitting by the fire with the orange flames in front of us, the photo is sublime. Another is where we are sleeping on lounge chairs facing each other, holding hands. And there was one last photo of Isabelle and me minutes before I left. I'm holding the compass in my hands, Isabelle is holding my hands, and we have our foreheads together, eyes closed as if we were praying or asking someone to make sure all this was just a nightmare.

"Wow, Maminou, these pictures are truly stunning. I deeply appreciate, immensely so, that you took the time to do this for me. You are really talented because no one ever saw you taking these photos."

"That was the point, too. I wanted to surprise you. And I aimed for the photos to be as natural as possible. Now you have some fresh pictures to put up on your bulletin board and a little memento of your friends from there."

"Yes, having something new on that bulletin board will be refreshing. I was just unsure whether to hang it back on my wall. I didn't feel like putting up the same old pictures again. Thank you, Maminou."

"You'll be able to take your own new pictures to add more." And she handed me a square package wrapped in beautiful pink paper with a big bow. "Happy early birthday, my dear."

"But why so early? My birthday is only next month, isn't it?"

"I know, but a month can sometimes seem long, and all this time, you can surely take a lot of beautiful pictures. The forest is full of wonderful surprises. Holidays are perfect for taking great pictures." her grandma replied with a wink.

I opened the package, and inside the box was an amazing camera with a memory card and two different lenses.

"Wow, this is so cool. It's my own camera. Thank you, Maminou, you're the best." And I hugged her neck and kept kissing her.

"I'm glad if it makes you happy. Shall we now fill those many feeders?"

"Yes, and I'll bring my camera to test it out." I took a few snapshots of Maminou filling the feeders, and some of the birds were already there, happy to eat. I could send pictures to my phone and send them to Isabelle. She congratulated me on my present and said we would take many together when she arrived.

We filled six feeders scattered around the yard: sunflower seeds and peanuts for the Cardinals and their mates. Thistle seeds are for the goldfinches, and a homemade mix is for the others, seeds of all kinds and dried fruits. Adèle even makes fruit skewers for the enthusiasts: grape, apple, orange, and kiwi. We could hear the birds singing and alerting their peers that the all-you-can-eat buffet had just opened. The squirrels came for the shelled peanuts, and it wasn't long before an incredible array of birds of all colors and sizes invaded the area.

"I think, Grandma, that we will need to refill them tomorrow. Given the number of birds here, we might need a whole truckload. I don't think your small bags will last very long."

"You're probably right; I'll buy more next time. But the swallows and others need to eat the insects around us too, or we will spend the summer indoors. And we must let nature do its job as well; they shouldn't just wait for us to feed them. The forest is full of food for everyone, and certain things must happen for everything to start anew. The bees must take nectar from the flowers to spread the pollen so that flowers, small fruits, and others can grow back. And so on."

"There will never be enough birds to get rid of all the insects living here. With this vast forest, there must be a tremendous amount of insects of all kinds."

"If you were aware of the number of flies a swallow can ingest in a single day and feed its offspring, you'd be amazed. There likely aren't many left by summer's end."

"I'm going to go for a walk in the forest. Will you join me, grand-Mi?"

"No, I'm too exhausted. I'll rest a bit, but please, don't stray too far. You're still unfamiliar with the area, I wouldn't want you to get lost." She could never get lost, but she doesn't know that, thought Adèle.

"Don't worry, I'll stop when I can no longer see the house behind me. Promise."

"All right, be careful, my little flower."

I set off to unveil the secrets hidden within this magnificent, vast forest. I followed a faint trail marked in the fallen leaves, surely trodden before. Oh, what a pleasant scent! The forest's moisture, the trees, the conifers, and the small flowers managing to grow despite the scarce light all concocted an intoxicating mix of aromas. I took several deep breaths, my lungs reveling in this pristine air. Turning around, I could still see the house in the distance. Yet, I felt I had covered a considerable distance, though it seemed like I had taken only a few steps. Humming, I looked up to see birds swinging on branches and butterflies landing on the leaves. I picked a wild mallow to taste. Grand-Mi also uses them in her medicinal mixes, claiming they make a revitalizing tea. What a treat. I love them in salads. Touching the trees, I felt as if sensing their life and breath. A noise. Footsteps in the dead leaves to my left.

"Hello, is someone there?" I asked, trying to peer around.

No answer. I looked towards where the sound originated, but nothing. I listened to the silence and heard nothing but the rustling of birds and the wind in the leaves; there was no one. Deciding to turn back, I figured it must have been an animal, perhaps a hare or a fox, that had darted away. Sounds can be plentiful in the forest. The footsteps were heard again.

It was indeed the sound of footsteps in the dead leaves. I turned around sharply and saw, as if a mirage, something moving in the distance in front of a tree. I also detected a scent at the same moment, a scent of plum roast.

"Who's there? Show yourself immediately. I can smell you. And I hear you." Fear began to scratch at my belly. My hands became all clammy. I took to my heels and ran as fast as possible, calling for my father. Indeed, they were ghosts.

"Dad! Dad! There's someone in the forest." Louis, hearing the vain cries, came to meet me.

"Lilou, what is it?"

"Dad, someone was following and watching me. It must be ghosts."

"What did you see?"

"Nothing, I just heard footsteps twice coming towards me, and no one answered when I called. And it smelled like plum jam toast."

"It's probably an animal."

"No, I'm sure they were human steps walking in the dead leaves. And animals don't eat plum jam."

"All right, I'll go and check with Grandfather. You stay here with your grandmother. And ghosts don't exist, Lilou, okay?"

"If you say so," I responded skeptically.

They came back a few minutes later, laughing, with their arms full of dead branches.

"There was no one there and no footprints. But we found some nice branches to make a great fire outside later with marshmallows and sausages."

"Okay, it must have been an animal then. I'm up for the fire. Shall we prepare the chairs and blankets, Granny?" Louis and grandfather were delighted that she had forgotten so quickly and hadn't asked any more questions.

The day passed very quickly. The dinner prepared by Mr. Henry was delicious and greatly appreciated. Ribs on the BBQ. Yummy!

"Mr. Henry, you are an excellent cook, and I genuinely relish having real meals. I was beginning to tire of pizzas and spaghetti with canned sauce from Dad."

"Hey, I make burgers and pancakes too," Louis retorted with a suppressed chuckle, causing the crowd to laugh. Mr. Henry took a moment to sit down to avoid falling from laughter.

"I'm really glad you like what I make, dear Lilou. I will happily cook all your meals. It's pretty much the only contribution I can truly make here for you. My bones are so old that sometimes I wonder if I'll be able to get out of bed the next day. I also enjoy tending to the rose bushes."

"I can't wait to see your roses and smell them. I noticed there were a lot of buds. They will be plentiful. May I make a bouquet for my room?" Lilou asked while enjoying a homemade sugar pie with vanilla ice cream.

"Of course, I always put a bouquet at the entrance and in the living room. I would be delighted to pick the most beautiful ones for your room. They should bloom in a few weeks. They were lacking a bit of presence recently. But you'll see, they are the most beautiful ones!"

"And you are not so old. Your soul is still very young, and so is your heart."

"Oh yes, my heart is still twenty years old."

Everyone helped Mr. Henry clear the table and do the dishes. We prepared coffee, tea, marshmallows, and sweets for the fire. Mr. Henry recounted old stories about the house and the families who lived there in the past. In front of the large fire dancing, yellow and orange, he told how, during the war, they hid people in the cellar to save them from certain death. How a British Colonel had taken over the house for several months to lead his regiment, and how the soldiers used the stable as a dormitory and depleted their wine stock and killed most of the cows and chickens for food. At least the homeowners could benefit from the food and some protection. The evening was very enjoyable. Mr. Henry is a great and very funny storyteller. He even grabbed a small beer to join Louis and Alfred. Adèle drank her tea, and I had my spruce beer. The bag of marshmallows was emptied in record time, and the grilled sausages were too. The deep blue, almost black sky was filled with stars. I listened to the sounds of the night. I was nearly asleep when the sound of a breaking branch startled me awake. Dad jumped from his chair, and Adèle spilled tea on her trousers. Mr. Henry gave Louis a questioning look. He gave him a very discreet negative sign.

"Get away, you filthy beast! We have nothing for you," Mr. Henry shouted so loudly that it scared me. "We should go inside, I think the nocturnal beasts are out, and the smell of the sausage must have attracted them."

Everyone entered the house without protest. Alfred and Louis went with Mr. Henry to store the ground chairs in the cellar.

"Why haven't you told her yet?" Mr. Henry asked Louis.

"I don't know, I think she's not ready," Louis replied, suddenly uncomfortable.

"She is not ready, or are you not ready?" Alfred asked.

"Ok, ok, it's me who's not ready. I just wanted to give her as much time as possible in a normal life."

"Her life is normal. What awaits her is just as much."

"There is nothing normal in this, Alfred: powers, an entirely scripted life, and a destiny carved out in advance. Every day she wakes up in the morning, each minute will have been foreordained. She won't have any freedom whatsoever. She won't be able to make decisions for herself anymore."

"What do you want to do? Tell her the night before the first day of school. 'Ah yes, Lilou, I must tell you that your school, where you must go tomorrow, is not like any other. There are animals everywhere to prevent Hades, the king of the underworld, from coming to harm you, and all the children in the school have powers. Some can vanish, others talk with animals, and even those can transform into the animal of their choice!'" said Alfred sarcastically. "'Oh yes, and I forgot, you are the future queen of nature and will have great responsibilities waiting for you. You must protect us all from certain death. And you have very great powers, you need to develop them.'" Said Alfred with a sarcastic tone.

"No, I wouldn't have told her that way."

"So how do you plan to tell her and handle her reaction quickly?" replied Alfred calmly. "There's not much time left, you know. Do you remember how you reacted when your father told you that you would be the future armorer and the Chief Architect of our combat centers, arsenal, and everything we would need?"

"Allow me to tell you that it's not just about telling her about the school but also admitting that she IS the power and our future Queen," said Mr. Henry to Louis calmly.

"I know, but I just wish she had more time," Louis said with tears in his eyes.

"More time for what?" Alfred was from the old school and didn't understand his reasoning. "In my younger days, when I was eight years old, we were trained according to our power. The boys had fun playing with swords and learning to make them. Girls either dealt with potions, different languages, or spells. They competed with those who could learn and master them the fastest and without errors. Sometimes, fixing the mistake took longer than learning it, but it was funnier too."

"More time in ignorance. In the innocence, in the pleasures of the life of a young adolescent. No more time not worrying about the future, with Hades wanting to destroy everything and the rules to follow. I want her to go through the little problems of a normal teenager. I want her to come and ask me about puberty, not how to stop the dark king!"

"I understand your concern, but failing to prepare her is to her detriment, especially since she arrived here. The animals sense her presence, and the forest creatures are aware of her arrival. They will seek to connect with her, and she might be terrified. Imagine a squirrel speaking to you or an owl transforming into a man in front of you, unaware such things exist," Henry explained, glancing at each of them one after the other. "That's probably what was in the forest today. They feel her presence; we will not be able to control them."

"You are right, Mr. Henry. I will talk to her tomorrow. I would like us to have breakfast together and be there to support her."

"Of course, we will be there and don't worry; she is Stella's daughter, and Adèle's granddaughter, and also Adélaïde's great-granddaughter. She will understand," Alfred reassured him, patting his shoulder.

They returned to the first floor to rejoin the women. As Alfred ascended the stairs, he recognized his wife's scent of dried flowers; she must be running a bath.

Louis didn't find Lilou at first.

"I'm off to bed, gentlemen, good night." Mr. Henry left through the back door, heading to his small house at the end of the garden. His golf cart awaited, and his legs could no longer walk the distance.

"I'll go see Lilou upstairs. Good night, Alfred. See you in the morning."

"Good night, my boy, and don't worry about tomorrow morning; we will all be there with you, and everything will be just fine."

"I sincerely hope so. Thank you, Alfred, and please say good night to Adèle for me."

Louis went straight to his daughter's room, knocking softly at the door. No answer. He knocked again, a bit louder.

"I am in the bathtub, Dad. Grandma gave me dried flowers to put in the water. She says it will help me sleep better."

"Okay, I wanted to check how you are doing."

"I'm good, but I got petrified outside. I'll come out and join you in your room in five minutes." Lilou hurried out to talk with her father. She wanted to go to bed immediately so she could get up early to walk in the forest before the day's heat set in. She had something to check.

Alfred entered his room. Adèle was indeed enjoying a relaxing bath. He knocked on the door softly.

"May I come in, my dear?"

"Of course, given the time we've lived together, you don't need to ask." He entered and sat on the edge of the bath.

"You look rather worried. What's the matter?"

"We were chatting downstairs while putting away the chairs."

"I noticed it was taking a while. I told Lilou you must have gone outside to put out the fire and ensure everything was fine outside."

"You did well because she might have overheard us. Louis wants us to have breakfast together tomorrow morning. He will talk to Lilou and would like us all to be there to support them both."

"Oh Lord, already the big day. Couldn't we wait for Isabelle to come and go? Let her at least enjoy this last normal pleasure."

"But what's with this obsession with normalcy? There's nothing abnormal. We are who we are, and we must embrace our true selves."

"Times have changed, my dear love. People today are different from our youthful selves. Back then, we had nothing to distract us other than practicing fighting. We had nothing but our wits and fists, striving to excel or concoct as many medicines as possible within a minute. Today's young people converse on devices as tiny as notepads, portable enough to take them outdoors with them and walk around. At Lilou's age, we didn't even know about television yet."

"I understand, but we must not descend into madness or overprotection for fear of making her even more vulnerable."

"Indeed, you're correct. Tomorrow morning is a good time, and she can discuss it with her best friend. Perhaps that will ease her acceptance." Alfred planted a kiss on his wife's forehead and exited the bathroom to retire to bed.

Louis pondered over managing the scenario. As dawn approached, the weight of the message weighed heavily on Louis's mind. What was he going to tell her? How could he convey tomorrow's message with words that would soothe rather than instill fear? His thoughts raced, pondering how to reveal to a soon-to-be 17-year-old the truth about her extraordinary destiny as the forest's chosen queen, gifted with unparalleled powers. And yet, her upcoming school held a secret community of peers, each unique in their abilities yet united in purpose. The enormity of the task threatened to overwhelm him as he paced back and forth in his room.

Just then, Lilou's entrance interrupted his restless contemplation. How could he articulate the transition awaiting her at 16, where childhood must yield to the weighty responsibility of guiding their collective survival into adulthood?

"Are you all right, Dad? You seem troubled."

"I'm perfectly fine, my dear. I'm just pondering over the noise we detected earlier. I hope it's not a large beast preventing our summer outdoor evenings."

"I'm quite sure they're more frightened of us than we are of them."

"Possibly. But, no bears reside here, so fear is unnecessary."

"It's not fear, but I thought I saw someone near the tree when I opened my eyes. When Mr. Henry shouted, 'Leave, we have nothing,' the figure vanished."

"What do you mean by vanished?" Louis inquired, anxious about her response.

"The entity or person, I'm unsure of what I saw, beside the tree just dissipated, evaporated."

"Come now, Lilou, you must have been dreaming. Vanishing is impossible."

"I know! I was almost asleep just before the sound of a breaking branch. I must have still been dreaming. But I truly felt I saw a man in the darkness." Lilou wondered if she was sleeping or if she had indeed seen that man standing in the forest's gloom. "How could someone become transparent anyway? The answer lies within the question. It was impossible, so I was still asleep."

"Come on, let's go to bed. A good night's sleep will set our minds straight. Tomorrow is another day, and we have much to do."

"Yes, you're right, Dad. Tomorrow, I would like to buy some paint to color my room before unpacking all my boxes."

The night was turbulent. Nightmares of transparent men coming to kidnap me, they were all black and faceless. Bears walking on two legs shouted at me to flee and said they would protect me. I woke up abruptly after feeling someone grabbing my ankles. My heart was pounding. I was drenched in sweat, and my hands were trembling. The clock showed five in the morning. I got out of bed. The coldness of the floor sent a shiver down my spine. I put on my bathrobe, turquoise, of course, and took a hot shower to warm up. Thirty minutes later, I was dressed and had my hair in a ponytail. I had my breakfast, peanut butter toast and a glass of milk. Dressed in my lined jacket and rubber walking shoes to stay dry from the morning dew, I stepped out of the house to explore the surroundings. The property is so large, so many things to explore. Which direction should I take? Let's go straight ahead. I reminded myself constantly to keep the house within sight, its gray walls a beacon in the distance. If ever I turned around and couldn't spot it anymore, I knew I had ventured too far. A simple rule kept me from losing my way and ensured a safe return.

As soon as I crossed the boundary of our property and stepped into the forest, I felt a tremor under my feet. A sensation of well-being, peace, calm, and joy overwhelmed my entire body. The smells, sounds, and perceptions of the things around me were heightened. When I placed my hand on a tree's bark, I felt it breathing. Breathing deeply, I advanced into the woods. I thought I could hear an ant eating a maple leaf. The myriad scents intoxicated my whole being.

I turned around and could still see the gray color of the house in the distance. But I was almost at the limit of where I could go. I leaned against a tree and momentarily closed my eyes to listen to the ambient sounds. I heard a noise behind me. Again, the sound of footsteps in the dead leaves of past autumns. I turned around but saw nothing. There was no one else but me. I took a deep breath and recognized the smell of fresh plum toast. I closed my eyes and listened carefully to all the sounds. A calm breathing and a heartbeat played the drum not very far from where I was.

"Who's there? I can hear you. Show yourself."

"I can detect the plum roasts you consumed at breakfast and perceive your heart, which seems quite agitated."

"All right, I will reveal myself only if you promise not to flee or be frightened."

"Why would I be scared?" she retorted to a male voice.

"Please, promise me."

"Okay, okay, I promise," I responded, shrugging my shoulders.

My gaze fixed on where the voice originated. I saw nothing, no one. Footsteps neared me. Then, as if by magic, a young man materialized before me out of nowhere.

Suddenly, I found it hard to breathe. I took to my heels and ran as fast as possible back home. I burst through the front door, slammed it shut behind me, and locked it.

"Dad, Dad, come quickly!" Alerted by her screams, Louis and Alfred rushed over.

"Lilou, what's the matter? What happened?"

"Are you hurt?" Alfred asked, out of breath from his quick dash from the far end of the house.

"No, I'm not hurt. You'll never believe me. I saw a boy materialize right in front of me."

"What? Appear, what do you mean? Where were you?"

"I was in the forest taking a walk, and I heard footsteps behind me. Like yesterday, footsteps in the leaves. I asked, 'Who's there?' And suddenly, a young man appeared like magic. I struggled to catch my breath. There was no one, and then, poof, there was someone. Just like that!!" I snapped my fingers to demonstrate the quickness of the appearance.

"Come on, Lilou, people can't just appear out of nowhere," Louis said, overtaken by panic. "How can we explain all this?" He cast a pleading look at Alfred, seeking his help. They had been unable to discuss it at breakfast as planned because she had left before they were all awake.

"You must have seen a mirage, the sun in your eyes, or something like that, darling. You know there's an explanation," Alfred replied, nudging Louis and looking him straight in the eyes, indicating it was time to tell her the whole truth. The forest sensed her presence, and they couldn't hide it for long. The forest dwellers would come to her one way or another.

"No, no, I didn't see a mirage, I really saw him appear in front of me. I know it all sounds bizarre, and I can't believe what I see. Dad, go outside. Go into the forest and try to find the boy I saw. He's about my age, taller, with dark brown hair and tanned skin. He smelled like fresh plums. He was wearing blue jeans and a white short-sleeved shirt. And I could hear his heart beating extremely fast. Like he was super nervous."

"What?" her grandfather asked, surprised.

"Yes, I could smell his presence before I saw him appear. He smelled like plum toast. And I could hear his heart beating."

"I didn't know you had such a keen sense of smell," Alfred said with a look and tone in his voice, telling Louis it was enough to tell her everything or that he would. The men looked at each other in silence.

"Do you remember Mr. Flore at the end of the street where we used to live? The one with lilacs in his yard?" I said to my father.

"Yes."

"Well, when I wake up in the morning, I can smell the buds blooming. When someone rings the doorbell, I can tell who's behind it before even opening it. I think I can smell something up to a kilometer away."

"Wow. I can hear conversations from a very long distance," her father suddenly said.

"Why didn't you tell me this before?"

"I don't know. I didn't think it was necessary at the time. I can also move objects." He moved the coat rack next to the entrance door with his right hand.

"That's amazing. How do you do that? Show me."

"You can't learn it, Lilou. It's like your odor. It's a gift."

"I can bring animals back to life, and I have the gift of potions," Adèle said with a big smile and a compassionate look. They turned to look at Adèle behind them. She was joining them, having overheard their conversation from the kitchen where she prepared potions and tea blends.

"How can you bring things back to life? That's not possible. It goes against nature."

"Yes, of course. Do you think I would lie to you? I know it's a lot for you all at once, but give us time to explain, and you'll understand everything."

"I don't think you're lying to me, but you can't bring back something dead. Come on, that's playing against nature."

"We call them gifts, my little wildflowers. And I think it's high time we had a good family discussion." She turned to her husband and took his hand.

"You're right, my dear. Let's go to the kitchen, have a bite to eat, and have a nice cup of tea. We'll need the energy. I think this discussion will be very long. Louis, the big day has come. It will be up to you to start the conversation. We'll be here to support you and help Lilou understand."

They all went to the kitchen. Adèle and I made toast and fruit. The men made tea and prepared a fire in the large living room. The place would be more comfortable for this kind of discussion. Alfred made a special tea for his granddaughter. He wanted her to be calm and her mind to be completely open to analyze and understand the meaning of what was going to be said. He searched through his wife's herbs to find an excellent blend to facilitate the discussion and help Louis find the right words to explain everything to his daughter and keep her calm. Louis put a lot of wood in the main fireplace to warm the room, which was still filled with the morning's dampness, and created a relaxing atmosphere. They laid breakfast and different teas on the large center table, and Adèle lit candles to relax the room. Lilou returned to the kitchen to get some towels and glanced out the window. Mr. Henry was talking to a young man at the edge of the forest. She took a couple of minutes to observe them carefully. It was the young man she had seen appear in front of her. He was about her age, even though he was taller.

"Come now, my dear, we are waiting for you." Lilou turned to her grandmother and gestured for her to come.

"Look, that's the young man I spotted in the forest. Mr. Henry seems to know him. Let's go see them, please."

"Later, let's talk first. You'll have plenty of chances to talk to him. He will be at your school next September."

"How do you know that?"

"Because all the young people from this area attend your future school."

"What do you mean? Is it like a cult or something?" I began questioning things and feeling anxious about what was coming.

"No, not at all, you'll understand later. For now, let's go to the living room to talk. You will see, it's a big piece of news we must share."

She picked up the paper towels she had come for and the plate of red grapes that was on the kitchen counter. Adèle followed closely, casting a final glance at Mr. Henry. We took our seats in a chocolate brown leather armchair near the fire. Alfred served us tea and a plate of toast with peanut butter and raspberry jam. At first, we ate in silence. Adèle and Alfred exchanged looks with Louis, who was staring at his plate. Poor Louis, how can he confess to his only daughter that her mother is still alive, that she is the queen of nature, and that she would have to replace her one day? How do we tell her that she possesses the greatest powers on earth and that the universe she has known until now is not the real universe that surrounds us? That animals can be transformed into humans. That trees can talk to us. That birds can understand us and that unimaginable creatures exist in the forest. He remembered when his parents told him he was an armorer and a great protector. He had to become an architect to design the weapons and shelters. One for every need. Lord, how he had wanted to disappear. Let's start by telling her that, he thought to himself.

"When I was your age, I was already madly in love with your mother. Nothing and no one could have separated us. When my parents told me that I was a protector, of the Arms and that I had to become an architect to construct future shelters or hiding places for our weapons. The only thing I wanted was to attend the same school as Stella. There was no question of separating from your mother; she felt the same. So when we learned we would be at the same school, we agreed to become everything our parents wanted. I was going to become the best Architect in my group, and Stella would learn all the spells, potion mixtures, and herbs by heart as quickly as possible. She was the best, and all the others were very afraid to face her in a duel, even me. If you had seen her, she was so beautiful and confident. The teachers often used her to give private lessons. She was superior to many of us and even to several Elders."

"What was her power?" asked Lilou with great interest.

... A slight hesitation.

Louis looked at Adèle and gestured for her to speak. He thought she was best placed to talk about it, since it was her mother.

"Stella is the Queen of the forest, my little wildflower." A heavy silence full of questions fell over them.

"The Queen of the forest? What does that mean? Is it like the Miss Universe pageants?"

"Oh no, it's much more serious than that. I was the Queen before her, and she succeeded me. She controls plant and animal life. She ensures that everything that dies regrows and that the balance of life remains as evenly balanced as possible. She also ensures that the dark side does not come to invade us."

"The dark side!?! Like Darth Vader in Star Wars?"

"No, my dear. Not quite. The darkness, hell. Hades is the King of darkness, and he wants to come to earth to reign and thus be able to release the lost souls in hell."

"You can't be serious?" Lilou looked around at everyone in turn. She couldn't believe a word of what her grandmother was saying. "You're kidding me. This can't be real. Queens who give life and madmen from Hell want to come to Earth to kill us. Are you crazy or what? Is this a belated April Fool's joke? Well, you got me there!"

"No, we are not crazy, my dear. Let us explain and show you what truly exists outside."

They talked for hours. Alfred, Adèle, and Louis demonstrated their powers. Mr. Henry entered the living room with a dead potted plant in his hand. He walked over to Lilou and handed her the pot. She took the withered flowerpot.

"What should I do with this?" Looking into his eyes, I noticed he had aged backward strangely. How is that possible?

"Sing to it the song you often hum in the evening as you prepare to go to bed," her father said.

She began to hum.

"Day chases after night. Night chases after day. They circle my yard, sleep tight, my friend." The flowers stirred in the pot. Gently, they came back to life, and in a few minutes, it was a small bouquet of pink roses, beautiful and fragrant.

"Wow, how did you do that, Mr. Henry? You are an excellent magician."

"I did nothing, my dear. It was you who brought it back to life." Louis's mouth hung open. He didn't realize his daughter already possessed such great powers.

"Me? But how could I have revived dead flowers?"

"You have your mother's powers. But even stronger. Much stronger."

"How do you know they are greater?" Alfred asked Henry. His own daughter had only managed that feat in her third year of secondary school.

"When she stepped out of the car upon your arrival, the earth pulsed with energy. I haven't felt that since your great-grandmother Adèle."

"How, you knew my great-grandmother, Mr. Henry?"

"This house has been in your family for eight generations, and I have known the last six." Lilou gave him a quizzical look, raising her eyebrows.

"How is that possible? You can't be 220 years old."

"I have seen many moons, that's true. The first Queen who lived here gave me the gift of agelessness and the ability to assume any desired appearance. I chose the appearance of an old man for you, thinking it would be more comforting." He turned away, his grey hair darkening. When he faced them again, he was about the age of Louis, her father. "This is generally how I look. I stopped aging when I was 38 years old and have a lot of history."

Lilou was speechless. She looked around at everyone in turn, and no one seemed surprised. Everything appeared perfectly normal, as if changing appearance at will was commonplace.

"No, it just doesn't make any sense. You're there, staring at me, waiting for my reaction as if I'm supposed to say something... I don't know what. Am I dreaming or what? Please, wake me up, I've had enough."

"My dear, everything is fine. Reacting like this is normal. We've all been through it before you. I ran away and never wanted to return to this family. I begged my friend at that time to let me stay with her. What I didn't know was that her parents were also like us. I still spent two weeks at her place, digesting what was happening to me, but then her father turned into a dog in front of me. I fainted. When I woke up, I realized that I couldn't change anything, that I just had to accept it and learn to control my powers."

"But I don't want to go to some silly school and learn magic tricks. I want to go to a school where they teach French, mathematics, and biology and be with other kids my age who are worried about their acne problems and whether their breasts are too small or too large. Wondering with which boy I'll have my first kiss and who will take me to the end-of-year prom. I want to experience ordinary and normal things." I ran off, taking the stairs two at a time, and slammed the door of my room.

The next morning, I woke up fully dressed on my bed. I couldn't even remember the day passing or going to bed the previous night. No one had disturbed me. They had preferred to leave me alone to think, and as my grandfather often said, "the night brings counsel." I went to take a shower, hot, very hot. I had no desire to go down to the kitchen. No one was there. Everyone was outside on the terrace enjoying the wonderful sun. I made myself toast with apple compote made by Mr. Henry the day before and went to join my family outside.

"Slept well?"

"Yes, I don't even remember touching my pillow. I missed the whole day."

Nobody was speaking. They were waiting for me to speak first, to ask my questions. I was pondering. I would have no choice. Such was my life. I settled myself on a sun lounger.

"Where is mom?" I asked the first question that popped into my head.

Dad was so taken aback by the question that his mouth fell open, yet no sound emerged. He looked at Adèle, and tears began streaming down his cheeks.

"What I am about to tell you will not be easy to hear, my dear," Adèle began, taking a deep breath. "Your mother, like myself before her, my mother and my grandmother, and all the women before us, are the queens of the forest. This entails many responsibilities that you will learn about later. The greatest challenge in becoming the queen is to protect our family. To better protect them, we must leave them. Distancing ourselves is the first step. That way, no one knows where we are, and they can't reach us by taking our family or children."

"Are you telling me that my mother is alive? But had to abandon me and never come to see me to protect trees and squirrels? And to stay away from me in case someone came to attack me?"

"It's not quite like that. Yes, your mother is alive. But she didn't abandon you to protect trees. It's more complex and significant than that."

"What's more important than watching her daughter grow up? Teaching her how to make pancakes on Saturday morning or how to apply makeup without looking like a clown at school? Or how do you shave your legs without having to walk around with bits of tissue stuck on the wounds to stop the bleeding because you cut yourself with the razor? Or what to do when you start your period. That it's not my fault, but rather completely normal when becoming a woman, even at ten. Explain to me what is more important because I don't understand at all," I screamed in rage, tears brimming in my eyes.

"If trees and animals still thrive on Earth, it's all due to Stella. Our very conversation owes itself to her presence. Hades, the dark realm's sovereign, perpetually schemes to seize the earth and forests to erect his abode. She must thwart his passage through the Erebe, the layer dividing us from the netherworld. In time, you'll inherit her role and grasp the magnitude." Said Adele with calmness.

"Never, I shall never assume her place. Look for another person for this burden. Father, if our stay here is imperative, I acquiesce, yet I shall not attend that school nor wish to unearth the powers you claim reside within me. Let no further mention of them reach my ears."

****

With July's onset, my room's confines became my world. Family meals were forsaken as I grappled with the deceit surrounding my mother's tale. How I yearned for a mother like Isabelle's, who, despite not being her biological progenitor, embodied the only maternal figure she ever knew. Their bond epitomized the quintessential mother-daughter nexus, encapsulating shared shopping excursions, muffin baking, and Isabelle's sewing tutelage, a stark contrast to the bond I yearned for. Louis, imparting lessons in self-defense and mundane tasks like oil changes and lawn mowing, excelled in fatherhood. My affection for him is profound, yet it remains a father-daughter dynamic. Grandma's unwavering presence, despite her culinary and household teachings, could never substitute for maternal intimacy. A deep breath unveiled the scent of wild berries, heralding Isabelle's arrival at the back door. Springing up hastily, I sent the lounge chair and sketch papers fluttering.

"Isabelle! I'd nearly forgotten that today was your arrival. Your presence fills me with joy!" Embracing her tightly, I noticed I had grown. I no longer needed to tiptoe for our embrace, a fleeting thought, perhaps.

"I thought this moment would never come. The last two weeks have been the longest two weeks of my life. And I thought my mother would never let me go. She cried as if I would never return home."

"It would be great if you could stay here and attend my school. I'll tell you about the school later. I'll have all summer to discuss it. For now, let's enjoy your presence. Let's take your bags up to your room. And then we'll go eat; you must be very hungry. Your room is just across from mine."

"I'm starving. Who's the old man who welcomed me at the door?" I was wondering who she was talking about. Mr. Henry looked like my father the last time I saw him.

"He's not old; he's about the same age as my father."

"What! But no, that's impossible. He has all-white hair and a bent back. He walks with a cane."

Ah! I was wondering if he would change his appearance like that every time a new person arrived. "Yes, of course, that's Mr. Henry, our handyman."

"He must not do much. He looks like he's 200 years old."

They burst out laughing and couldn't help but laugh all day, imagining Mr. Henry in funny ways, considering his age. July passed very quickly. August was approaching too fast for the girls.

"Let's take a walk in the forest, Lilou. Why don't you want to go? Are you afraid of the little bugs that live there?"

"No, I'm not afraid. You wouldn't believe me if I told you why I didn't want to go."

"Of course, I'll believe you, come on. We've never lied to each other and always told each other everything. Whatever the reasons are for not wanting to go into that forest, you can talk to me about it."

"I don't even know where to begin. And you're going to think I'm crazy."

"Never in my life. Just start wherever you want. Wherever you think you should start. But tell me. Lilou, you look strange. I've never seen you like this. You're trembling. Tell me everything. Tell me what scares you."

I paused, gathering my thoughts before I spoke. "You know," I began, "There's a whole world out there that most people don't see. Creatures, magical and mysterious, living deep within the forest's embrace. And me, I have a gift. I can breathe life back into wilted roses, turning them into vibrant blooms again. Then there's my mother, not just any mother, but the Queen of our enchanted realm."

"Lord, my dear, have you started taking drugs or something?"

"No. You see, I told you that you wouldn't believe me. This house has been in my family for eight generations. My mother is the guardian of nature, and my father is an armor protector. He can move objects, and my grandmother can bring a dead animal back to life."

"Wow! What you're telling me is completely insane! You can't bring something back from the dead."

"I said the exact same thing when they told me about it a few weeks ago. And you want to hear the best part? The school I have to attend in September is for kids like me. It's a kind of wizarding school, like Harry Potter. We thought those movies were just fiction! No, I have to learn how to make potions with herbs and control my mind to hear what others are thinking."

"What you're saying, Lilou, is completely insane. You're starting to scare me a little. But why do you absolutely have to go to this school?"

"Because one day, I'll have to replace my mother and save the flowers and the bees," she replied sarcastically.

"All of this makes no sense. Is that why your sense of smell is so developed? Because you have powers?"

"Yes, I can also hear very distant sounds. I can feel the life in the trees and hear the animals talk to me. I can't talk back to them. They respond to me, but I don't understand them because I haven't been initiated yet."

"Initiated! What is that?"

"I have to receive the sacred water from my grandfather and undergo the welcome ritual. I don't understand how it works and didn't want to hear about it. I was in shock and didn't ask any more questions."

"Okay, I see. After drinking this water, will your appearance change? Will you become a goddess? Will your hair grow to the ground and lose the even more sunlit wheat color? Will you be able to understand the languages of the animals afterward?"

"How did you guess my hair and everything else would change?"

"Really! Is that what's going to happen to you?"

"No, come on. Nothing will change, nothing noticeable to the eye. But my powers will grow as I learn to control them. I do not suspect many new powers will come, and I will have to learn a multitude of potions and herb blends by heart."

"And does that mean your mother is alive? That she just left like that one morning? Because she's a Queen! So you think you will see your mother again?"

"I don't want to see her. She abandoned me over ten years ago. She never called me for any of my birthdays. I never even received a card. Maybe I can't change anything about my future, but I can control my present, and I don't want to see her again."

"But maybe she had a good reason to leave."

"There is absolutely no valid reason to abandon one's child and definitely not to save trees, flowers, and mosquitoes. She made her choice. I am making mine. I will face my future with courage and determination, but I will never have children if it means that one day I have to abandon them to save nature in my turn."

"Wow! So maybe vampires do exist, and a handsome young vampire like Edward will come to take me in my sleep and carry me away into the night."

"You're dreaming, Bella. Vampires don't exist!"

"How do you know, huh? Yesterday, you didn't know you could talk to animals and hear a maple tree breathe. And I bear the same name as his beloved... Isabelle, Isabella, Bella!"

"It's not the same thing. No fantastical creatures exist. It's just nature as we know it."

"Like in the fairy tales, my mother used to tell me at night to put me to sleep. Sleeping Beauty and the prince's kiss. Or Snow White and the poisoned apple. Trees that breathe and raccoons that will tell you there's not enough dandelion for their breakfast. What's normal about that? All this is unreal. Come on! So, I say we don't know what else is alive in the world we are unaware of."

"Anyway, you can dream about your Edward if it helps you sleep, but I want nothing to do with vampires. I simply want to be me, a normal me."

****

July passed by too quickly. Louis, Adèle, and Alfred had decided to cease any school discussions with Lilou for the time being. They allowed the girls to savor their vacation time together. Seldom had they ventured into the forest, fearful of what might lie within. They often went shopping in town, consuming incredible ice cream. But as August began to emerge, Lilou was compelled to consume the sacred water in preparation for the significant return to school. Completing the initiation required time. Adèle and Alfred arranged the setting in the large living room. They placed a white candle for light, a white cloth for purity, and a fire for natural warmth. Louis readied his only daughter. She had to be dressed in white cotton, her hair tied back in a ponytail and bathed beforehand with a soap her grandmother crafted from pure, earth-sourced ingredients. These were hand-picked, fresh ingredients: goat's milk kindly provided by a generous neighbor to Adèle, wildflowers, and Lapacho tree sap. No perfume, jewelry, or makeup was allowed. The body had to be as natural and pure as possible. In a large leather chair in a corner of the living room, Isabelle was visibly agitated. Nervousness set in. With sweaty hands, she watched her best friend's grandparents prepare the living room table and light the fire.

"Could I do something, please? Could I light the candles? I'm nervous. I can't stand sitting here waiting anymore."

"Of course, darling, go ahead and light the candles, but you must say a little thought for Lilou when lighting each one. Ideally, each candle should have its thought, but it's okay if you use the same one more than once."

"Okay." Isabelle wondered what she could say for ten candles. Perhaps ten different prayers? 'Go ahead, my dear. You can find ten positive thoughts for your best friend.'

First candle: 'Bring peace to Lilou, please.

Second candle: 'May calm accompany her throughout her life.

Third candle: 'I wish for her never to feel fear.

Fourth candle: 'May her powers be majestic.

Fifth candle: 'May she become the greatest protector this world has ever known.

Sixth candle: Isabelle glanced around to see if anyone was watching her before uttering the next one. She didn't want to be heard for this one. 'May she be the most beautiful girl in her school and have all the boys crazy about her.' She said quietly with a smirk.

Seventh candle: 'May she remain my best friend forever.

Eighth candle: 'May I stay here and go to school with her to protect her. This one might not be entirely for her, but a little bit since it's to protect her.

Ninth candle: 'May she accept and forgive her mother. Who I'm sure had good reasons for leaving her.

Tenth and last candle: 'May everything go great.' Isabelle said a little prayer inside before handing the matches back to Adèle. She prayed to her parents, her birth parents, to help them, to surround her best friend with wisdom and kindness. She thanked them for giving her life. 'I sincerely believe that my place is with Lilou. I can't say why, but I have a feeling that I have to stay with her to protect her. If what I feel is true, please ensure I can stay here and attend this school with her. Thank you.'

"There, I've lit the candles with a prayer for each one. What else can I do?" she asked Adèle.

"Would you like to do the ritual with Lilou? Would you like to be initiated, too? You never know. Maybe there's a gift inside of you? And since you turned 17 already in June, it's perfect."

"Oh yes, I want to. I know I don't have a gift, but I would love to share this moment with my best friend. Thank you, Adèle. But is everyone okay with it?" Isabelle asked Louis and Alfred for their approval.

"Of course, my dear, come with me. We'll get you ready." Adèle took her by the arm, and they went to Adèle and Alfred's bathroom since Lilou was in hers. "You need to take a bath to purify yourself with a soap I made from natural ingredients, like flowers, tree sap, and honey."

She explained the whole process and brought her a white dress for purity. After the bath, Adèle brushed her hair and tied it into a ponytail, placing a white flower in it.

"There, you're ready. From now on, you're not allowed to speak. You only have to answer our questions. No questions, no comments. You must clear your mind and accept what will be given to you.

Before going down, do you have a question? Because after you pass through that door, you must not say anything else. Even when you see Lilou, you must remain silent. Do you understand how important this is?"

"Yes, I understand very well, but my question is, why do I have to clear my mind to accept what will be given to me? I'm not like you. I don't have any powers."

"Because you're special to Lilou and us," Adèle exclaimed, "the Goddesses will welcome you into the family. You'll be part of our large family after this ceremony." Adèle was convinced that Isabelle had a gift, even though they had never seen any signs. Considering her biological parents were great warriors, it's impossible from her experience for two parents of the same kind, two warriors born of warrior parents themselves, to conceive a child without any gifts, no matter how minimal. Generations usually inherit the gift from their family; it's hereditary. The gift can change. There have been cases where two warrior parents conceived an animal child, able to take the form of any animal they choose or have a completely different gift like speaking with animals or controlling temperature. The Goddesses decide the gift based on current or future needs. But Isabelle cannot have any gift. It's high time she knows the truth about her parents.

Isabelle knew her current parents were adopted and that her biological parents had died in a supposed car accident. But she didn't know she already belonged to our family and who her birth parents were. They had died protecting Lilou's mother from Hades, the king of darkness. They died heroes, preventing Hades from crossing the boundary between darkness and the surface of the earth, the Erebe. Everyone was here today because of them. Adèle couldn't wait to tell her but had to keep quiet for now. 'You never know what happens in the first sleep after initiation. Great things can happen. But one thing at a time.' Adèle thought to herself.

"Are you ready?"

"Yes, I'm ready. I hope I'll have the gift of changing people's minds. That way, I could convince my parents to stay here to accompany Lilou to her school."

"Ah! I didn't know you wanted to go to that school?"

"It's so she won't be alone and to protect her from gossip. She's never been able to be mean to ignorant or foolish people and tell them off, but I have," she said with a big smile.

"I know, you've always been the one to defend her since kindergarten."

"Yes, and believe me, they would say hello to her afterward and then run away. I don't know why I've always felt the need to protect Lilou. I couldn't explain it. It's a feeling inside me."

Adèle took her hand with a big smile, and together, they went to the living room to join the group waiting for them.

Upon arriving at the living room, Lilou learned from her father that Isabelle would experience the initiation with her. The surprise on Lilou's face was absolutely indescribable. One could almost read the questions on her forehead because her eyes spoke so much.

"You have to light the ten candles for Isabelle. Each candle should have a thought just for her. A positive thought, an encouragement, whatever you want."

... Lilou nodded to indicate she understood. She couldn't speak anymore. 'Wow, ten different thoughts.'

1. 'I wish Isabelle would stay here with me.

2. 'I hope Isabelle can accompany me to my college.

3. 'May she find her own Edward. Lord, I need to think of something brighter.

4. 'May she discover a great talent.

5. 'May joy and happiness always be by her side.

6. 'May each new day be better than the last.

7. 'May all the boys be madly in love with her.

8. 'May this initiation bring her great surprises.

9. 'I wish for Isabelle to have a beautiful life. She deserves it.

10. 'What else could I ask or wish for her?

Please help me make the right choice. She closed her eyes and heard someone whispering in her ear, "Ask the Gods to keep her by your side to protect you and that she has the possibility to meet us in her dreams tonight so we can tell her the truth about her origins."

"But who are you?" I asked in my mind.

"I am Anna, Isabelle's mother and a close friend of your mother, Stella."

"Okay," she made her wish for Isabelle. She thought she would have plenty of time later to ask her father or grandparents about the voices she had heard and Isabelle's origins, her best friend.

The ceremony went wonderfully. The girls were initiated according to the rules and drank the sacred water. Isabelle and Lilou looked at each other, wondering what would change in them or if anything would change. They glanced at each other, hoping to see a change in some way. Alfred recited several prayers, made gestures over their heads, and one by one, they drank the last sips of the sacred water. Isabelle felt something strange inside her, as if something was growing. But it must be the result of wanting something so much that she was having illusions. Lilou felt a calm and incredible sense of well-being.

She felt like she could fly if she jumped out of the house. A huge shiver ran through the girls at the same time. It was as if a strong draft had come in through the window next to them. Even their hair fluttered a bit. Alfred stopped for a moment, surprised by this realization. He had felt that cool breeze pass by. He looked at Adèle and nodded, indicating she was right about Isabelle. She had a great Gift. He didn't know what it was, but he was eager to find out.

Mr. Henry, in his tranquil corner, watched the girls and thought that Adèle was right to initiate them at the same time. Isabelle was ready for the truth as well. He felt their presence. Her parents were close by and waiting for the right moment to appear. Tonight would be the night. Having drunk the sacred water, she would be able to see them in her dreams and better understand what they were going to tell her. Lilou stood up. Her knees were like jelly. She stretched her arms to the sky and took a deep breath. The air didn't smell the same anymore. Her skin was hypersensitive.

"Well, my beauties, the ceremony is now over. You are now part of the great family of Earth's protectors."

"Congratulations!" Mr. Henry exclaimed. "Let's eat and drink now. Girls, I've prepared your favorite meal, four-cheese macaroni. For us, I've prepared dill and lemon chicken. I also made a fantastic cheesecake with strawberry coulis. Come on, let's enjoy ourselves." Adèle put on some music, and the men grabbed a beer. The girls made themselves fruit cocktails. The party continued into the early hours of the morning. Lilou was falling asleep. Isabelle was struggling to keep her eyes open. Louis put his daughter under his arm and led her to bed. Adèle took off Isabelle's white dress as she sat on the edge of the bed and undid her ponytail.

"Tonight, you will have wonderful dreams, Isabelle. You will meet people you know and be able to talk to them. Tomorrow, you will never be the same. Tonight will make you a completely different person. But above all, you will learn things about yourself that will serve you in your future."

"All right, thank you, good night..." She didn't even have time to finish her sentence before she fell into a deep sleep. Her breathing was calm and relaxed.

"That's a good thing," Adèle thought as she pulled the blanket up to her neck and kissed her forehead. She left the room gently, closing the bedroom door behind her. Adèle had lit incense sticks, pine gum, fragrant spices, and orange peels to promote Isabelle's sleep and concentration. The encounter she was about to experience tonight would be the most important of her life.

Isabelle was dreaming. She was standing in a forest. It must have been around 1-2 in the morning because the moon was high in the sky, illuminating everything as if it were daytime. She walked a little to see where this path would lead her. The moon was shining as brightly as the midday sun. She had never seen a moon so clear and luminous.

"Isabelle." A soft, faint voice called her name.

She stopped in her tracks. Someone was calling her from behind. She was afraid to turn around. She kept moving forward.

"Isabelle, Isabelle. Stop and turn around. Don't be afraid," the voice said gently.

Isabelle closed her eyes for a few seconds. A ball of nervousness formed in her stomach. She turned around to face the woman's voice that was calling her. When she opened her eyes, the woman standing in front of her was not alone. A tall, sturdy man with jet-black hair stood beside her. Strangely, she felt like she had seen them somewhere before.

"Hello, Isabelle," the woman said with a big smile. She was radiant, with long blonde hair and eyes of a dazzling green, looking almost identical to Isabelle.

"Hello," Isabelle replied hesitantly.

"Hello, do you know who we are?" the man asked, looking her straight in the eyes. He had a very masculine voice, yet incredibly gentle at the same time.

"No. I think I've seen you before but don't know where. I don't understand how I can dream of you! Where are we?" Isabelle replied.

"We are in your dream, thanks to the sacred water you drank during your initiation today. And we are in the forest behind the house," the man explained.

"How do you know I was initiated today? And who exactly are you?" Isabelle inquired. The man was tall and sturdy, with a dark haircut that was very short.

"We have a lot to tell you, Isabelle. You need to stay calm and wait for me to finish explaining before you speak, okay?" the man said in a very gentle and calm voice.

"Okay, I'm calm. Actually, I don't think I've ever been this calm in my life; it's even strange," Isabelle remarked.

They explained to her that they were her deceased parents from more than ten years ago, Anna and Mike. They hadn't died in a car accident like her adoptive parents had always told her. That explanation had just been easier to tell. Now that she was about to enter college and had been initiated, she needed to know the truth at all costs.

"Yes, that's right, in photos. I've seen you in photos. It's been a long time since I've looked through my scrapbook. But you look a bit different," Isabelle said.

"Yes, we always look slightly different when we cross over to the other side of the wall. We're about ten years older than in the last photo you have of us," the man explained.

'Okay, but why lie to me all this time?" Isabelle asked.

"We were awakened in the middle of the night by Adèle and Alfred about 15 years ago. You were only two years old."

"Do you know Adèle and Alfred?"

"Yes, we know them very well. Adèle is my mother's sister." Isabelle took a step back. Questions flooded her mind. "I know you have a lot of questions, but you must let us finish before we can't talk to you after tonight. Don't worry. We'll answer all your questions after our story if you still have any questions. But I must finish before sunrise, and we only have 3 hours left."

"What do you mean? I don't understand. How can you talk to me as if we were in real life, and in 3 hours, I won't be able to see you in my dreams anymore?"

"We're not really in a dream. It's like a parallel life, like a second world. It's a bit like sleepwalking," her father explained. "The water you drank earlier allows you to see one or more people only once, on the first night following initiation, to gather crucial information about your future. During my initiation, I saw my grandfather, who taught me how to make weapons all night and a fantastic homemade beer. Your mother saw her grandmother, Adélaïde, who taught her potion blends, important healing creams, and her extraordinary chocolate cake. Back then, people fought to taste it."

"So after tonight, I won't see you again. I won't have known you, and I can only see you for about 3 hours one evening. That's not fair."

"I know, my dear, if only you knew how much we would love to stay with you and see you grow up. You are the most beautiful thing we've ever done. We love you very much. Please remember that we truly love you," Anna said, tears in her eyes. She stepped forward and reached out to Isabelle. "My name is Anna, and this big guy is Mike. You're so lovely." She introduced herself to her daughter as if for the first time. It was like their first meeting. Isabelle was so young when they died. She had no memory of them. Besides a few photos in her memory album, she didn't know her parents.

Isabelle watched her mother's hands, wondering if she could feel them or if they would pass through like a ghost. She reached out and felt Anna's soft, delicate hands in hers. They looked into each other's eyes, and Isabelle threw herself into her mother's arms.

"Mama!"

An immense feeling of comfort filled her body. Her father embraced the women in his life for the first time together in his strong, muscular arms. They were all crying, but immense joy burned deep within them, along with tremendous happiness. It was an inexplicable sensation, both sad and happy simultaneously. Isabelle saw her mother rocking her and her father playing the guitar while singing her a lullaby in a pink and white room. She understood that her parents were passing on memories to her that she would always cherish. She savored their scents, hoping to remember them upon waking. They stayed embraced for a while, then sat on the ground near a massive oak tree. Isabelle was in the middle, and they continued their conversation.

They explained that they had given their lives to save Stella, Liliane's mother, The great Queen of the forests. The night an attack of darkness suddenly awakened them, they entrusted their daughter to their neighbor. They were just ordinary humans, but they knew their secrets. They were extraordinary people who, unfortunately, couldn't have children. "They filed for adoption the day after our deaths. They wouldn't allow you to live with anyone else. We knew you would be in good hands, and Adèle, Louis, and Alfred would always watch over you."

"How do you know all this?"

"We can see and hear you but can't communicate with you. You can talk to us; we'll always be by your side. But we can never respond."

"Are you ghosts who haven't crossed over?"

"Oh, you can see it that way. We don't move into the afterlife. We always stay here. It's like a parallel world."

"It must be difficult to see the people you love aging or facing problems, illnesses, without ever being able to do anything."

"Yes, it's very difficult, but at least we can see you grow up." They didn't want to tell her right away that there was a way to talk to each other. Not right away. She would learn it at school. It was too much for one night.

"Are you always next to me? You don't watch me undress or when I enter the shower, do you?"

"No, of course not. We respect privacy, and we're not always by your side. We have things to monitor and people to follow. The darkness doesn't sense our presence; we can watch and observe their every decision."

"How do you do it?"

"We stay close to their lairs and listen. When we have important information to convey, we go to the queen's mother and transfer our information to her."

"The queen mother? Who is she?"

Mike and Anna exchanged looks for a second. Should they reveal who the queen's mother was? Had Liliane been informed about her mother?

"The queen mother is Stella, Liliane's mother." They were waiting for Isabelle's reaction.

"Oh, yes, of course. Liliane found out she was still alive. She thought she was dead. She doesn't want to know anything about her and absolutely does not want to see her."

"We weren't sure if she already knew. Her reaction is completely normal. She'll change her mind over time. One day, she'll need her, and Stella will come running."

"I don't believe so," Isabelle said. "I saw the anger in Lilou's eyes. It's sporadic for Lilou to get angry at someone; that's usually my job. I know Lilou very well; when she says no, it means no. And when she's angry, it takes a long time for her to calm down."

"Let's not waste time talking about Liliane and Stella, please. We have very little time left," Mike said eagerly, holding his daughter tightly.

"You're right. We only have one night with you, my dear, and we have so much to tell you."

"Yes, let's make the most of it. And by the way, it's not Liliane. It's Lilou. She hates being called Liliane."

As the sun tickled Isabelle's nose, she slowly opened her eyes. She wanted only one thing in that moment: to fall back asleep at all costs. "Go back to sleep, go back to sleep," she whispered to herself, squeezing her eyes shut. Isabelle wished she had more time with her parents. She knew she would never see them again.

"No, no, no!" she cried out loudly. Adèle hurried over with Lilou.

"What's wrong, Isabelle?" they both asked in unison, kneeling by the edge of the bed.

"I saw my parents last night, and I'll never see them again. I was only allowed that one night. It's not fair. I never got to know them, and now I'll never see them again."

"You saw your parents? I saw my great-great-grandmother Céleste. Your grandmother Maminou. She told me so many things and said to accept that my mother couldn't be with me. That is our destiny, and you all did the same before her. It's the sacrifice we make so that others can exist and survive. Did you do that, too, Grandma? Did my mother grow up without you?"

"Absolutely. I've been fortunate enough to see her a few times, as things were much quieter in my time. My mother before me could be at home sometimes. Everything suddenly became more complicated. I had to leave during Stella's 8th birthday. The darkness began to understand how to return to Earth and take shape, maybe even stay. We lost many families and friends that year. We had to rebuild almost entirely with children the same age as your mother and others with a few years' difference. Like your parents, Isabelle, they had to age quickly and learn all the basics of their powers: potions, creams, powders. Both to heal and to harm. We had to prepare for the next attack of darkness. We knew that even though we had defeated them once, they would come back even stronger. We had observed their weaknesses. I also understood how to defeat and slow them down. But so did they. The young people of this generation did not have a childhood. They worked day and night all their lives to defend and protect us. You can ask your father, Lilou.

That's why he waited so long before telling you. He wanted you to have a childhood. An adolescence full of obstacles, laughter, and sorrow. A true love pain. A real young girl's life. All the people of his generation did not have the right to. You must forgive your mother. That's why I took her place in a way. So she could protect all of us. Your father learned to forge a sword before even knowing how to write. He didn't know why; we didn't want to scare them. We said it was a game and that weapons were for hunting. They had to make enormous sacrifices to preserve life. Your parents, Isabelle, sacrificed themselves to save Stella from the hands of Hades. They plunged into the darkness so that Hades wouldn't return to Earth. Until this day, he never succeeded in coming out of his black hole. Your parents' lives saved all life on Earth. Adults, children, animals, and plants. Without them, we wouldn't be talking right now."

"Wow. Isabelle, you're one of us. We're alike. And your parents are heroes."

"Yes, we're cousins, but I don't have any powers myself."

"It may be true, but you're also my best friend. That's something, right?" she said, laughing. "Maybe that's why we love each other so much. We're from the same family. It's really great. Cousin."

They burst into laughter. Everyone at breakfast that morning had something to say or questions to ask. It was a very long meal. Mr. Henry had regained his natural demeanor. Now that Isabelle knew everything, he could return to being the 38-year-old man he had always been for so long. That day passed quickly. The sunset came as if by magic. The girls lay on their backs in bed with their eyes open for a long time. It's been a very long time. Isabelle thought of her father, he's handsome. Tall and strong, with a bronzed complexion and muscles ready to explode. She only thought of her parents. They slept deeply that night. No one came to visit them or disturb their sleep. They needed to recharge their energy. Tomorrow was another day. Lilou and Isabelle would have incredible encounters, and their lives would never be the same again. Louis and the grandparents left very early that morning. The girls went to the kitchen for breakfast, and only Mr. Henry was there.

"Where is everyone else, Mr. Henry?" Lilou asked.

"They must have left very early to take care of some things for school and had errands to run in town."

"I would have liked to go to town too. They could have waited for us to accompany them," she said, disappointed that she couldn't go shopping.

"No problem, Miss Lilou, I can take you and Miss Isabelle there. I have some provisions to pick up myself," Mr. Henry said with a big smile. "I think there will be a lot of people here on Saturday," he said mockingly. "I seem to recall that someone's birthday is coming up very soon! There will be surprises... Did you think we forgot about you?"

"I love surprises," Lilou said excitedly, dancing and clapping her hands. "I'll get dressed and be ready in 5 minutes."

Isabelle chimed in as she climbed the stairs two by two. "Me too." The girls raced each other, reaching Mr. Henry like synchronized swimmers. They had a great morning shopping and running errands. Of course, they stopped for ice cream before heading home. Isabelle got her usual pistachio, and I chose black cherry. Mr. Henry, who prefers simplicity, opted for a soft serve vanilla.

The week flew by.

****

Turning seventeen was going to change a lot in my future life. First, finally, high school. Five years of secondary school were enough. In some places around the world, primary school lasts six years, not counting kindergarten. At the same time, for us, it's seven, besides changing schools for high school, which is in a different building than primary, and then another school for grades 8 through 11. And now college, but not an ordinary one, I've been told, no more French, geography, or math like other teens.

Instead, I'll learn about potions and antibiotics that can sometimes regrow a hand, for example. I'll learn about my powers, how to control them, and most importantly, how to grow them. I'll need to know about others' powers to know who to contact when needed. I'll also learn swordsmithing. A Queen must be able to replace anyone in case of war. And, of course, I'll learn to speak with animals and assist them in their progress. That's what my future will look like, our future. We won't become nurses. I'll have to choose a cat, just like Isabelle. Everyone must have a cat because they sense the presence of the departed and can communicate with them for us. That's how Isabelle will continue to communicate with her parents. She'll learn this on her first day of class. Cats also sense the approach of darkness. If someone tries to breach the door that separates us from darkness, all the cats start meowing, and their fur bristles. Everyone can hear their meows, like an alarm signal that lights up in people's bodies. Even if you don't have your cat near you and no cat nearby, you hear it or feel it. It's an alarm signal that no one can miss. It's a connection formed with the choice of our cat. But they choose us rather than the other way around.

Saturday morning. I opened my eyes and felt a presence in my room. I closed my eyes immediately and tried to guess who was there. I took a deep breath, and the smell reminded me of something, but I couldn't remember where I had smelled that scent before. I quickly sat up in bed when my brain replayed the memory of that smell. My mother was sitting in the armchair by the window. She looked so beautiful. Wearing a long emerald green dress with light veils, her hair the color of bark, long down to her lower back.

Long, slender fingers and green eyes with a hint of orange sun. Just like me. Perfect skin. I didn't know what to say. I didn't want to see her or talk to her. Stella waited patiently. She didn't want to be the first to speak. We looked at each other for a moment. Suddenly, the door to my room opened. Both of us looked at the door in surprise. They all came to wake me up, singing Happy Birthday. The astonishment on my father's and grandparents' faces at that moment was indescribable. Stella stood up from the armchair and looked at Louis. This man she loved so much, she hadn't seen in so long. He looked handsome in his blue pajamas. His muscles are even more pronounced than before. They looked at each other for a moment, and Stella threw herself into his arms.

"I didn't know you were coming back today," Louis said, burying his face in his wife's hair. He loved her scent so much. She smelled like freshly cut grass, dew, and wildflowers in the morning.

"I've been waiting for this moment since the day I had to leave you. There was no question of waiting one more day. I'm sorry I didn't warn you, but I was afraid of leaks."

"It's okay, the surprise is really pleasant." He kissed his wife tenderly and buried his nose in her hair again. He couldn't believe she was finally back.

Adèle and Alfred hugged them, and Stella turned to her parents, whom she hadn't seen in a very long time.

"Mama, papa, I'm so happy to see you again. I missed you so much. Time felt so long."

They hugged and kissed each other. Stella turned to invite Liliane to join in for hugs. She wasn't there anymore. She had left the room through her window, using the lattice as a ladder to climb down, and they hadn't even heard her leave.

"But where is she?" Stella went to the window to look outside, but there was no sign of her daughter.

"Give her some time," said Louis. "She'll come back. It's a lot for her in such a short time. Learning who she is, the initiation, finding out Isabelle is her cousin, and you appear in her room when she believed you were dead all these years."

"Yes, let's go downstairs for coffee and lunch. She'll come back. She can't go far in pajamas." Adèle was the first to leave Lilou's room and pulled her husband by his robe sleeve. He looked at her with question marks in his eyes, and from her gaze, he understood.

"We'll join you in a moment." Louis pulled Stella's arm and kissed her passionately. Their breathing quickened, and Louis' hands tried to rediscover his wife's perfect body.

"Mmm, my sweet, I almost forgot how beautiful you are. I missed you so much."

"I missed you too. But now I'm here to stay. I'm not leaving again. That's out of the question."

"I completely agree with that."

Two hours had passed since Liliane's sudden departure. Isabelle had come down for lunch and was introduced to Stella. She wasn't sure if she should curtsy, kiss her hand, or say hello. Adèle saw her confusion and gestured for her just to say hello.

"I'm going to get dressed, and then I'm going for a walk in the woods to try to find our runaway. I'll bring her a jacket and some shoes," Isabelle said.

As soon as the attention shifted to Stella, I left the room, grabbing only my jacket and slippers. I walked straight into the forest without looking where I was going. Tired from walking, I saw a water reflection in the distance through the trees. I picked up my pace. I had never come this far into the forest before.

Wow, I couldn't believe my eyes. This place is beautiful, almost magical. There's a big rock a little further ahead, and I was going to sit there. The weather was still a bit damp and chilly. The sun was just rising, and you could still see the morning dew on the leaves and grass. My slippers were soaked. Rainbow-colored birds came to bathe. They took a bath and smoothed their feathers. Slowly, more and more animals were around me and in the water. In the blink of an eye, there were more than I had seen in my whole life. I smelled a familiar scent: plum toast.

"I know someone's here. I can still smell you. You smell like ripe plum toast. And I can even tell you they're blue plums." She didn't turn around and waited. Footsteps behind her were getting closer.

"Hi," said a male voice.

I turned around slowly, and a bolt of lightning ran through my body as our eyes met. It was as if I was now connected to this person.

"Wow, you're a nature girl too?" said the young man, feeling the electric shock pass between them.

"What? What are you talking about? And who are you?" I asked.

"Hi, my name is Inaky. Didn't you feel the lightning between us?"

"Yes, but what's a nature girl?"

Inaky suddenly wondered what to reply. If she wasn't already aware, it wasn't for him to inform her.

"Who are your parents?" He asked.

"My parents! Louis and Stella. Why?"

"Stella is your mother? The great guardian of the forest is your mother?" He took a step back. He knew she had powers; he could sense it, but he didn't know she was Stella's daughter.

Lilou didn't understand his question and how he knew her mother, whom she barely knew herself. "I'm not sure if we're talking about the same Stella," said Lilou.

"She came into your room last night. In fact, she's been there since you fell asleep. Is she really your mother?"

"Apparently, yes."

"I know what you're thinking. 'She's my mother, but I haven't seen her since I stopped sleeping with Mr. Tranquille, my teddy bear. She abandoned us, and suddenly, she appeared in my room on my 17th birthday. I don't want to talk to her, and I don't want to know anything about her.'"

"How do you know my sleep buddy was Mr. Tranquille? And how do you know what I'm thinking?" she said, a bit angry. Was he spying on her for a long time? She wondered. "Who are you?"

"Oh no, I'm not spying on you," Inaky replied. They both stared at each other, eyes filled with questions.

"Okay, I can read minds. And often, I hear what people are thinking without being able to stop it. One of your powers is smell, right? Do you have another power?"

"I have no powers."

"Of course, you can feel I've devoured toast with plum jam from miles away. And you sensed my presence when no one else had before. Don't be afraid. I'll show you something, okay?"

"Okay."

Suddenly, Inaky vanished into thin air. I felt his breath on my neck. I turned around, and there he was. He was standing behind me. He's really cute, I thought to myself silently, with his tanned skin and ebony-colored hair. His delicate nose, corn-colored eyes, and candy-pink appetizing lips.

"How do you do that?" I was genuinely surprised and curious at the same time. I punched his shoulder to see if he was also transparent.

"Hey, I'm human, just like you. That hurt. I become transparent, but I'm not transparent."

"I wanted to check. How do you do that? Were you the one I heard in the forest the other day? How long have you been spying on me? Are there others like you? And what else do you do?"

"Stop! Let me answer. You're bombarding me with questions all at once, and I don't have a second to answer them. I can't explain how I do it; it's my gift. I was born this way. Yes, it was me in the forest. I sensed your arrival, just like all the animals and living beings here. I'm not spying on you. And yes, there are others like me with different gifts. You'll see, at school, we're all different yet all the same."

"How can one be different and the same at the same time?"

"What I mean is, we all have a gift, but they're not necessarily the same. We're like a family. Children from the same family resemble each other, but they're all a bit different. So, for us, it's the same thing."

"I'm a bit scared to go to this school. I don't know anyone, and I don't even know myself. I don't know what my gift is. I don't know what I can or cannot do. I'm very nervous."

"Well, now you at least know one person at this school."

"Are you going to this school for the first time like me? And are they all like you? What grade will you be in?"

"Yes, also 1st year. The first year here like you. Do you want me to accompany you on your first day? It would make me very happy. And no, all students have a gift or a different specialty. Some look alike but have different things too."

"That would be very kind of you." I extended my hand to him. "By the way, I'm Lilou." We shook hands, and a second electric current passed from our hands to our feet. I even had a shiver in my hair. We looked into each other's eyes for a moment. I felt like time had stopped. The animals were all around us, silently observing us. It was like a scene from Sleeping Beauty when she meets the prince in the forest by the riverbank, and he dismounts from his white horse. Just as I felt like Inaky was going to kiss me, I heard footsteps and recognized Isabelle's scent. Our heads turned at the same time towards Isabelle, who was coming out of the woods with her head down and froze in place. Isabelle's eyes went from me to the stranger. Stunning, tall, with corn-yellow eyes, but who has yellow eyes? Yellow eyes don't exist except in the Cullen family. There was a silence that seemed really long. Isabelle felt like she had broken an important moment. She looked at me and didn't know what to say.

"Your parents are looking for you and starting to worry," Isabelle said timidly, not daring to look at the boy with yellow eyes.

"Is Stella still there?"

"Yes."

"I'll wait for her to leave before going in," I said, turning to Inaky. Knowing he could read my thoughts, I stared him straight in the eyes and said, "Isabelle comes from protective parents. She went through the initiation trials with me to accompany me. But go easy on her, please. Just like me, she's not used to all this. She was adopted after her parents died fifteen years ago. But by humans without powers. Did you understand me?" He nodded slightly in agreement.

"Hey, I'm Inaky. I live just on the other side of the forest," he introduced himself, extending his hand and waiting for Isabelle to respond.

"Hi, I'm Isabelle, Lilou's best friend. I'm here on vacation," she said, staring at his yellow eyes like tiny grains of corn. "How can you have yellow eyes? Yellow eyes don't exist. It's not possible!"

"Yes, I come from an owl family," he said seriously without hesitation, waiting for her reaction.

Isabelle burst out laughing. She looked at him and realized he wasn't laughing at all; he was as serious as a pope. She glanced at Lilou, who didn't know how to respond. Isabelle stopped laughing and questioned Inaky with her eyes.

"My parents are from the animal family. They can transform into owls. Not me, but I inherited their eyes, allowing me to see in the dark like daylight. It's convenient. Lilou is from a natural family; I think she'll be able to talk to animals and hear them when she's ready. She'll probably also be able to control the earth and all its elements, like water, fire, air, and earth." He looked at the girls in turn, who stared at him with mouths wide open in disbelief and surprise.

"This is all too much for me in such a short time," Isabelle said, closing her mouth and shaking her head, hoping to regain her composure. "Last night, I met my parents in a dream as if it were real. I found out I come from a family of protectors. Now I understand why I always felt like I had to protect you, Lilou; it's in me and my blood. And now you're telling me some people can turn into owls. And why are there so many animals around you anyway?"

"They come to meet our future Queen. Her coming here has stirred everyone up. The forest is already more alive thanks to you, Lilou."

"What are you talking about?" I asked.

"You. You are our future Forest Queen. Your mother's replacement one day. Who replaced her mother and so on. It's your family. You are the Royal family."

"Never. I will never be your Queen, firstly because I have no power and secondly because I'm not interested in supposedly leaving my family to protect the world and its insects. And thirdly because... because... I don't know why, but I just don't want to, that's all."

"It's true that it's a lot to take in so quickly. Anyway, it's not tomorrow that you'll have to replace her. You have to be trained and complete your initiation journey."

"Yes, and I'll also have time to grow up and decide for myself."

"Let's go back, Lilou. You must be hungry, and your family will start worrying."

"Yes, you're right. See you later, Inaky?" I said, hoping to pick up where he might have been about to kiss me.

"Yes, of course. Just say my name, and I'll appear."

Timidly, they parted ways, and Inaky watched her walk away. When they entered, the house was very quiet. Lilou heard low voices in the large living room. They headed towards the kitchen, where Mr. Henry was preparing lunch.

"I'm very happy you're back, Lilou. Shall I prepare a snack for you?"

"Please, Mr. Henry. I needed to be alone and think." He nodded in approval. "I met Inaky. Do you know him?"

"Ah, charming young man. He lives on the other side of the forest. He used to help me sometimes with carrying wood for the fireplaces and other small tasks. I like him a lot."

"We kind of had an electric shock when we first met. It was bizarre." Mr. Henry paused from cutting fruits momentarily and looked me straight in the eyes.

"You felt an electric shock. Did you feel like time stopped for a moment? And were there many animals around you at that time?"

"Yes, absolutely. How did you know that, Mr. Henry?"

"I don't know, I just wanted to know." He continued cutting his fruits and flipping the eggs in the pan. He understood that Lilou would be a powerful Queen and that Inaky was meant to be her partner for life. He is her other half. Nothing in the world would separate them. Nothing and never. It's like that for us. It's like that for the great Goddess. They have soulmates like Adèle and Alfred, Stella and Louis. They are always the same soulmates who come back but must find each other in the next lives. They always find each other.

Later in the day, the girls were outside in the courtyard, lounging on a deck chair. Music in their ears, sunbathing, what more could two 17-year-olds ask for? Isabelle turned 17 back in June. Louis pulled up a chair next to his daughter and tapped her shoulder, gesturing to remove her headphones with his index finger. She took off her headphones and sat up a bit, adjusting the reclining position. She knew what her father would say and didn't want to hear it.

"My beautiful princess, I know you're very angry with me, your mother, and maybe your grandparents too. But you have to let your mother explain and talk to you. She didn't have a choice but to leave, you know. I was separated from her too all these years. You seem to believe you're the only one who suffered from her absence. Do you think it was easy for me to raise you alone, knowing that your mother was somewhere fighting the madmen of darkness without me? To do everything to give you a normal life and to keep you from knowing anything about it until the last day of your 16th year. No, nothing has been easy. Plus, you became the best friend of the daughter of the parents who saved your mother and all life on earth. It was complicated to hide all this from you and to act normally every day for all these years. You must give her a chance. Anyway, she's staying with us, so you'll have to face her and have a mother-daughter discussion sooner or later."

Isabelle had turned off her music to listen. But she pretended the music was still playing by moving her feet to an imaginary beat.

"Not today, anyway. She abandoned me. She made the decision to leave me without a mother and go live in a tree and wait. She'll see what it's like to wait for someone who doesn't come."

"She didn't have a choice, Liliane. We would all be dead today if she hadn't left. You'll have that responsibility one day and won't have a choice. Isabelle's parents didn't have a choice either. They sacrificed themselves to save us all and save their daughters, or we would all have died. We're here right now having this conversation thanks to Anna, Mike, and Stella." Louis raised his voice. He had never raised his voice to her before today.

"You never call me Liliane. I will never have to make that decision because I refuse to be what I should be. Or rather what you want me to be. Find someone else because it won't be me." I immediately put my headphones back on and turned up the volume. I closed my eyes and focused on the music. I could hear my father talking, but I didn't want to continue this conversation. My decision was made.

"You owe me that much, my daughter. For protecting you from the truth all this time so that you could have a wonderful youth." Louis put his head in his hands and turned towards Isabelle.

"Isabelle talks to her. She will listen to you. Try to make her understand that Stella didn't choose to leave. She had to leave, or we wouldn't be having this discussion right now. Hades would have taken control of the earth, and it would be hell here right now instead of a quiet court on the edge of the forest. Your parents passed away to save us, and I'm truly sorry for you, my dear. Lilou needs to understand that. Tell her she will listen to you more than me."

"Okay, I'll talk to her later. But how did you know I was listening?"

"You are her protector, Isabelle. It's in your nature," replied Louis, heading back inside.

Lilou's birthday was great. It was a bit ordinary due to the lack of guests, but still fun. They invited Inaky to eat outside with them, having burgers and hot dogs on the BBQ. Gifts, music, lots of treats, and Lilou's favorite dessert as a birthday cake. A three-tiered cake, three colors, with buttercream frosting, just as her Maminou knows how to make it. Chocolate, white, and pink, like the three-color ice cream.

"Thank you so much, everyone. Thank you, Maminou, for the cake. Thank you, Inaky, for being here too. And thank you, Stella, for finally being here for one of my birthdays," she said sarcastically. Stella had a tear in her eye but turned her head to hide her pain from her daughter.

"Do you know that Inaky is, I believe, Lilou's soulmate?" Henry asked Louis.

"No, why do you say that?" Louis replied curiously.

"They had an electric shock when they held hands the other day. Lilou told me about it. I didn't tell you anything." He said, looking into Louis's eyes. He didn't want to break the trust Lilou had in him.

"Okay. I won't say anything to anyone. Let's wait and see."

****

July is already over. It's already mid-August. Isabelle, Lilou, and Inaky became very good friends. They saw each other every day. They played hide and seek in the woods with other teenagers that Inaky had introduced to the girls before school started. They will all go to the same school.

Inaky cheats all the time. One day, while we were in the woods, I had to find Isabelle, him, and the others. I wanted to play a trick on Inaky to teach him a lesson. If I were the future Mother Nature, I would surely control her or ask her to do things for me. I was looking for where Inaky was, and I felt his presence behind a tree very close to me, and he was still transparent, the rascal. I froze, closed my eyes, and asked the tree to hit him with a branch. Not hard, just to surprise him. I thought it wouldn't work anyway because I had never learned to do that. I saw something bounce in the air, and a loud scream broke the silence.

"Ouch!" Inaky landed in the dead leaves a few feet from where he was hiding. Isabelle, who was climbing in the tree nearby, almost fell off the branch in surprise.

"What happened? Who did that?" Asked Inaky without addressing anyone in particular and getting up.

"I think it was me," I replied in shock. "I wanted to teach you a lesson because you cheat all the time. I asked the tree to give you a little tap with a branch just to surprise you. I didn't ask it to throw you. Anyway, I never thought it would work."

"You wanted to teach me a lesson! This is really funny! But how did you do that? You've never received any training. There are people who try to do that all their lives, even after many trainings or teachings, and they can barely move a leaf."

"I don't know, I just said in my head, give him a little tap with a branch, please, and the tree propelled you to the other end."

"Wow, you'll be super powerful. I think you'll be the most powerful Mother Queens ever seen. Your mother holds incredible records, you know. But I think you'll beat them so easily, blindfolded and with your hands tied behind your back," Inaky said, jumping with joy. He was very excited.

"Lilou, you will be the best." Isabelle was still in shock yet so happy for her friend at the same time.

I was very happy to have managed to move the branch. I think I should maybe be careful about what I ask for in case I hurt someone. I said to myself.

One day before the big return, Isabelle stays one more day with her friend. She didn't want to leave. At lunch, the silence was very heavy in the dining room. Even though the room was immense, we felt like the walls were closing in on us. Louis entered, followed by Adèle and Alfred.

"It feels like we're at a funeral home," Louis remarked. "Girls, I have something to tell you." They looked at Louis with their eyes sad. "Isabelle has to leave today, and I would even say immediately..."

"Why? We still have one more day to be together. You can't take that away from us." Lilou almost shouted, cutting him off and standing up from her chair in fury. She stood in front of Isabelle as if to prevent anyone from taking her and bringing her elsewhere.

"I know all that, but she..."

"No. She's not leaving today." Louis had never seen his daughter angry. It was almost funny.

"Lilou, it's going to be okay. Don't worry. Everything will be fine. We'll see each other again during the next vacation, and we'll talk every day via video calls." Isabelle said, taking her friend's hand to calm her down. She had always known how to calm Lilou and protect her. How would she do that now, miles apart?

Adèle looked at Louis, pleading with him to stop this before the big tears came.

"Isabelle has to leave right away..."

"No, it's no. I had to move here because you decided it. I got initiated because you decided it. I have to go to this damn school because you decided it. But look at me now because it's NO. Isabelle won't move from here."

"Stop and listen to me. She has to leave with Adèle and you to buy your school supplies for the start in two days." The two girls didn't quite understand what Louis was saying.

"But I don't have the same school list as Lilou. I can't buy my school supplies here. I don't have my list with me and no money," Isabelle replied.

"It's true that your list is a bit different from Lilou's, but it's still almost the same. You won't need a potion cauldron for your first year."

"What are you talking about, Dad? Our school lists will be completely different. I don't even have algebra math as she will have for the infirmary. I have to buy flowers and spices, birch bark, and snails. I don't even know what for. Snails, what good are they?"

"For their saliva. When they move, the snail leaves a trail of very sticky saliva, and we collect it to make ointments. This saliva heals almost all wounds. Especially burns."

"Ew! Okay, but I still don't understand about Isabelle," Lilou said impatiently.

"Well, after a long discussion with Stella, me, and your grandparents, we asked Isabelle's parents to allow her to stay here and go to school with you."

"WHAT!!!" The girls clung to each other and looked at the three adults in front of them with eyes filled with water and stars.

"Yes, Isabelle will stay here with us and go to the same school as you, my dear. We believe she should go to this school because she's part of the family. And since she comes from a family of protectors, she must have something hidden in her. We would love to be there to discover it with her."

"Hooray, hooray, hooray," the girls shouted, dancing in circles like children. They hugged Louis and kissed Adèle and Alfred.

"Don't forget Stella. She initiated the discussion with your parents, Isabelle."

Lilou turned around and saw her mother at the entrance of the dining room. She's really beautiful, she thought. She was leaning against the door frame with her large sunflower-yellow dress.

"Thank you, Stella," she said with a smile. Her mother felt a pang in her heart that she wasn't called Mom. But she understood. She had hardly ever spoken that name.

"I'm really happy for you two. Can I come shopping with you? It's been a long time since I went shopping."

"Yes, of course. Thank you very much. I don't know how to show you how happy I am to stay here. I'll protect your daughter well. You can be sure of that," Isabelle said, taking her best friend's hand.

"I'm sure of it. Let's go; we'll be gone for the day."

*****

Inaky was waiting for Lilou at the edge of the estate, behind the large tree-shaped gate that blocked intruders from entering. He spotted Isabelle by her side.

"What are you doing here? Weren't you supposed to start school yesterday?" Inaky asked.

"Yes, but I decided to accompany Lilou on her first day at the wizarding school," Isabelle replied.

"We're not going to a wizarding school. We're not wizards," Inaky stated.

"I know, but it reminds me of Harry Potter when he finds out he's a wizard and goes to his first day at Hogwarts. Except he goes by train, which is much cooler than the yellow school bus," Isabelle explained.

"Did your parents really let you miss your first day of school?" Inaky couldn't believe his ears.

"No, but I decided to stay anyway. Since they're far away to pick me up, I thought I would have time to be there at least for the first day before they drag me back by the scruff of my neck. Then we'll see," Isabelle said, struggling not to laugh.

"But her parents said yes. They didn't have a choice if you had seen the anger Isabelle showed. Even I was scared," Lilou added.

Inaky looked at the girls in disbelief as they walked towards the bus stop that would take them to school. He tried to read Isabelle's thoughts. Nothing. Complete darkness. He tried Lilou. She kept repeating, 'chocolate or cherry cone, chocolate or cherry cone.'

"Why do you keep repeating chocolate or cherry cone?" Inaky asked.

"Why are you trying to read my thoughts?" I retorted.

"I wanted to check if you're kidding me! Why do you have such a big backpack, Isabelle?" The girls exchanged looks and turned to face Inaky.

"I'm going to the same school as you. My parents allowed me to stay here and go to school with my best friend."

"You got me good! But that's great. Wow, you must be really happy. Anyway, I'm delighted." Lilou noticed a funny smile on his face. Was he interested in Isabelle?

After the summer we just had, I greatly appreciated Inaky. I feel good in his presence. I don't know what my reaction would be if Inaky was interested in Isabelle. The bus arrived, and there were already many young people inside. We all went in and followed Inaky, heading to the back of the bus. He sat next to a handsome young man who Isabelle really liked. A young girl occupied the bench next to them.

"Could you move to another bench, please," Isabelle said in a very authoritative tone, polite but authoritative. Already, Isabelle was showing her colors. "Move to the front bench. There's only one seat, and we're two." The girl went to the front bench without saying anything. Everyone was looking at Isabelle and me, wondering who we could be.

Thank you very much, Isabelle, for drawing attention to us. I said to myself.

Most of the young people on the bus have known each other since kindergarten. And for some, even before that. Everyone was talking quietly, all asking the same question.

"Who are the two girls with you, Inaky?" the young boy next to him asked.

"They're Lilou and Isabelle. They live in the estate."

"In the estate! So, they're from the Royal family?"

"Yes, they're from the Royal family, as you say."

"Can you introduce us?" he asked, getting off the bus. The school was really not far from the estate. They could have walked, but it was forbidden for security reasons.

"The girls, let me introduce you to Evan. He can influence your thoughts and make you say things you wouldn't want to say. He can also make you cry like a baby in front of your teachers."

"You try that on me, and you'll regret it, I swear," Isabelle said, advancing towards him with her finger pointing straight at his nose.

"That's the best introduction you've ever given me, Inaky. Thanks a lot for my reputation. They'll never trust me now."

"My grandmother always told me that trust is earned over time. You just have to prove that we can trust you," Lilou replied. "I'm Lilou, and she's Isabelle. We're new in the area and at school, too."

"It's nice to see you, girls. Inaky here disappears whenever he feels like it and avoids discussions when they get too serious. Or, he likes to scare people by breathing in their ears while being transparent," Evan said, a slight smirk on his face, proud of his revenge.

"We experienced this phenomenon this summer while having fun in the forest. Except I got my revenge. Isn't that right, Inaky?"

"Yes, yes. She hit me with a tree branch," Inaky explained to Evan.

"How did she do that?" Evan asked, curious.

"She asked the tree to hit me with a branch."

"But how? Nobody can do that except Stella, the Mother Queen. Nobody can control nature, especially not before the third year of middle school."

"I know, but she's her daughter." Inaky suddenly looked uncomfortable, realizing he had made a serious mistake. His face turned pale. "I'm sorry, Lilou, I didn't mean to reveal your secret. I apologize."

"I really thought I could trust you. I don't want people to treat me differently because of someone I don't even know," Lilou said.

"I won't say anything, I promise," Evan replied. "No one else heard what Inaky said. And I won't repeat it to anyone. He didn't mean to."

"I know he didn't mean to, but how many times will he slip up? I don't want people to know me by another person's name. I want them to get to know me and appreciate me for who I am, not for who I'm associated with. For my jokes or stupid mistakes," she continued.

She stared Inaky straight in the eyes and silently walked into the crowd to find her way through this massive school with stone walls. A multitude of steps led to a gigantic entrance. Large, heavy wooden doors with a design I didn't take the time to observe opened just as I arrived. A bell rang simultaneously. Several ding-dongs echoed. Every teenager had to present their finger at the door. I didn't understand why. A girl explained to me that we had to identify ourselves at the door so it could recognize us each time we entered. That way, no unauthorized person could enter the premises. I presented my index finger to the door, and it pricked my finger and absorbed my blood. I entered slowly, not knowing what to do, and waited for Isabelle, who went through the same process. On each side of the entrance inside, there were doors. On the left, one of them was a huge hall with large tables of old wood and benches that looked like park benches. It must have been the cafeteria. On the right, it looked like a gymnasium. On the left wall was a large staircase leading to the upper floors, and on the right, a long corridor with several other corridors and several other doors. Oh my, I'm going to get lost for sure.

"She'll forgive you. Give her time. She already has difficulty forgiving her mother for abandoning her and suddenly reappearing. Give her time. You're the first friend she trusted. And that's a lot all at once. Just a few weeks ago, she was an ordinary girl who thought she had an extraordinary sense of smell and that we would become nurses together. Now, she has to learn to save the world."

"She will never forgive me for betraying her," he lamented.

Starting a new school year will be much harder than I had imagined, I said to myself. I shared a locker with Isabelle because she had kicked the other girl out and gave her locker number. When Isabelle asked her politely if she could switch places with her, she strangely agreed without saying anything.

"You see, I'm changing. I'm becoming more diplomatic," she proudly exclaimed.

"That's true, bravo, you're making a lot of effort. But what if she had said no? What would you have done?" I asked her calmly.

"I would have probably asked her to leave before I got angry. Nicely. And with a big smile," she said, adjusting her hair and checking her makeup in a tiny mirror.

"And if she had cursed you or something?"

"I would have said, 'You change lockers, this one is ours. Thank you very much for your kindness.' And I would have turned my back on her."

"Isabelle, you can't do that all the time. That's intimidation," I said to her, warning her.

"I know, but I don't like it when people say no to me, so…"

"Please, you mustn't do that anymore, okay?"

"Okay, okay, I won't do it anymore. I promise," she said, crossing her fingers behind her back.

"Do all the young people here have a special gift?" Isabelle couldn't believe her eyes. There was a school full of special people.

"Yes, yes. She hit me with a tree branch," Inaky explained to Evan.

"How did she do that?" Evan asked, curious.

"She asked the tree to hit me with a branch."

"But how? Nobody can do that except Stella, the Mother Queen. Nobody can control nature, especially not before the third year of middle school."

"I know, but she's her daughter." Inaky suddenly looked uncomfortable, realizing he had made a serious mistake. His face turned pale. "I'm sorry, Lilou, I didn't mean to reveal your secret. I apologize."

"I really thought I could trust you. I don't want people to treat me differently because of someone I don't even know," Lilou said.

"I won't say anything, I promise," Evan replied. "No one else heard what Inaky said. And I won't repeat it to anyone. He didn't mean to."

"I know he didn't mean to, but how many times will he slip up? I don't want people to know me by another person's name. I want them to get to know me and appreciate me for who I am, not for who I'm associated with. For my jokes or stupid mistakes," she continued.

She stared Inaky straight in the eyes and silently walked into the crowd to find her way through this massive school with stone walls.

A multitude of steps led to a gigantic entrance. Large, heavy wooden doors with a design I didn't take the time to observe opened just as I arrived. A bell rang simultaneously. Several ding-dongs echoed. Every teenager had to present their finger at the door. I didn't understand why. A girl explained to me that we had to identify ourselves at the door so it could recognize us each time we entered. That way, no unauthorized person could enter the premises. I presented my index finger to the door, and it pricked my finger and absorbed my blood. I entered slowly, not knowing what to do, and waited for Isabelle, who went through the same process. On each side of the entrance inside, there were doors. On the left, one of them was a huge hall with large tables of old wood and benches that looked like park benches. It must have been the cafeteria. On the right, it looked like a gymnasium. On the left wall was a large staircase leading to the upper floors, and on the right, a long corridor with several other corridors and several other doors. Oh my, I'm going to get lost for sure.

"She'll forgive you. Give her time. She already has difficulty forgiving her mother for abandoning her and suddenly reappearing. Give her time. You're the first friend she trusted. And that's a lot all at once. Just a few weeks ago, she was an ordinary girl who thought she had an extraordinary sense of smell and that we would become nurses together. Now, she has to learn to save the world."

"She will never forgive me for betraying her," he lamented.

Starting a new school year will be much harder than I had imagined, I said to myself. I shared a locker with Isabelle because she had kicked the other girl out and gave her locker number. When Isabelle asked her politely if she could switch places with her, she strangely agreed without saying anything.

"You see, I'm changing. I'm becoming more diplomatic," she proudly exclaimed.

"That's true, bravo, you're making a lot of effort. But what if she had said no? What would you have done?" I asked her calmly.

"I would have probably asked her to leave before I got angry. Nicely. And with a big smile," she said, adjusting her hair and checking her makeup in a tiny mirror.

"And if she had cursed you or something?"

"I would have said, 'You change lockers, this one is ours. Thank you very much for your kindness.' And I would have turned my back on her."

"Isabelle, you can't do that all the time. That's intimidation," I said to her, warning her.

"I know, but I don't like it when people say no to me, so..."

"Please, you mustn't do that anymore, okay?"

"Okay, okay, I won't do it anymore. I promise," she said, crossing her fingers behind her back.

"Do all the young people here have a special gift?" Isabelle couldn't believe her eyes. There was a school full of special people.

"Yes, and the teachers too. It's unbelievable, isn't it?"

In the hallway, the young ones were sending pencils flying, clouds appeared above their heads, and papers shaped like butterflies fluttered all around. It truly felt like being in a movie. 'It's unimaginable.' The day passed by quickly. I sat at the front of the bus on the way back home. I didn't want to see Inaky, let alone talk to him. We crossed paths in the corridors, and I kept looking down each time. I'll never forgive him. He betrayed my secret. He betrayed me. Isabelle stayed silent and followed me onto the bus. She'd let me speak first. We did our homework together in the dining hall, face to face. We had sheets and sheets to fill out about our families, their powers, and our past experiences. Mr. Henry had prepared a snack of fresh fruits and freshly squeezed orange juice for us. I think he found us very quiet on the first day of school.

"Well, children usually have more to share on their first school day. How did you find it?"

"Huge. I got lost several times. I even almost peed in my pants, trying to find the bathroom. The teachers are all very kind and very interesting. I think I'm going to love this place. I'd rather learn how to mix herbs to make tea than learn algebra, arithmetic, or even worse, geometry or physics," said Isabelle.

"But you'll have to do geometry and physics, my dear. You'll learn them in different ways and for different reasons."

"Okay, but I'm sure it'll still be more interesting."

"And you, Lilou? How was your day?"

"Good. Thank you for the snack, Mr. Henry."

I stood up and left the room.

"I'm going to my room, Isabelle. See you at dinner time."

"Okay. I wanted to go for a walk in the forest, won't you come with me?"

"No. I'm not going to the forest today. See you later." I left the room and went to lock myself in my bedroom.

"But what happened to her today, Isabelle? I've never seen her like this before."

"Her friend, Inaky, betrayed her trust. He didn't mean to, but I think he really hurt her. He revealed that she was Stella's daughter. She hates that."

"I understand. I know Inaky very well; he's a nice boy. He'll apologize, I'm sure, and she'll forgive him."

"He's already done it several times. I think it will take her longer to forgive him because she's in love with him."

"Ah! It's not the same then. And you, is there a young man you fancy?"

"Yes, there's this Evan, but he influences thoughts, so I'm afraid he might influence mine, and deep down, I might not find him interesting for real, but only because he wants me to!"

"Evan, the little rascal. Once, he made me say yes so he could eat a blueberry pie all by himself. I told him that if he did it again, he would have to redo what he had asked us to do. Double."

"I'd like to see him make a pie. I'm going outside. I'll be back in about an hour."

As Isabelle left the house, she looked up at her friend's bedroom window to see if she was sitting there. She was perched on the window sill with headphones on, appearing to be writing or drawing. She turned her head upon seeing someone below. She greeted Isabelle and looked away. Isabelle understood she needed some time alone, so she headed into the forest. She went to the clearing where she had first met Inaky. The sun was splendid, and the warmth was perfect. No humidity, no wind. Inaky sat with his back to her on a large rock by the water, his pant legs rolling up, soaking his feet in the cold water of early September. He heard a noise behind him and disappeared instantly.

"It's me, Inaky," said Isabelle. "Don't just disappear like that; I want to talk to you."

"I didn't hear you walking in the forest. You startled me. Are you alone?" he asked, looking behind her.

"Yes, I'm alone. She will need time to forgive you. She trusted you, and you talked about it this summer. She hates it when people talk about her mother, especially when they compare her to her mother or assume she's like this or that because she's Stella's daughter. Lilou never talked about her. I've known her forever, and we never discussed her mother. For her, her mother was dead, and she would never come back. Today, she learns not only that she has powers but also that she comes from a very powerful family. That her mother is the Queen and didn't die but had to leave her to save trees and animals."

"I understand, but I never meant to hurt her. On the contrary, I realized I was wrong as I said it. I won't do it again. Evan will never tell anyone. He can change people's minds to make them believe what he wants, but he's not a liar or a bad person. He knows the difference between having fun making someone say funny things and respecting others."

"I know, but put yourself in her shoes. On the first day of school, the first person you introduce her to, and you reveal who she really is. Without giving her a chance to introduce herself, it puts enormous pressure on her, and people will expect her to be extraordinary. Super powerful and a prodigy. Lilou may not have great powers; she may only have her own powers, without being what people expect of her because she's Stella the great Queen's daughter."

"You're right. I hadn't seen it from that angle. I don't think people will expect her to be a prodigy. I should try to apologize again. Do you think she'll want to listen to me?"

"I don't think so. Not today, anyway. She didn't even want to come for a walk with me because she knew she would run into you."

"Hmm! I came here hoping to meet her to talk."

There was a silence for a long moment. Isabelle gave him time to think and dwell on it all.

"Evan finds you very pretty, by the way. He asked me if I had a boyfriend. I told him probably not, since you spent the summer here with us and are staying for the school season."

"Oh, I don't have a boyfriend, but tell him I'm not interested."

"Why? Don't you find him attractive?"

"Yes, he's very handsome. But I don't want him to influence my thoughts and make me do what he wants like a puppet. Without me even realizing it."

"Evan would never do such a thing. He's very respectful, you know. He's done silly things before for fun, but never anything mean. He never influenced, for example, a teacher for he's grade on an exam or his parents. He did with his parents once, but it was to get them to say yes to going out when he was grounded. But it wasn't mean."

"How would I even know if what I do or say with him is really my thought and not his?"

"Because he doesn't do that with his friends. He might make you say, 'I love bananas' when you hate them for fun. But that's as far as he would go out of respect for you."

"I don't know. I don't think I'll have time for a boyfriend anyway."

"Yes, and the year is young. Give yourselves time to get to know each other. Maybe you'll fall madly in love with him or someone else."

"Okay, well. Anyway, Lilou, she's in love with you, I think," said Isabelle to him, looking at Inaky with wide eyes.

"You think so?"

"I'm almost certain. I think that's the main reason why she's having a hard time forgiving you. She's never loved a boy before, you know."

Inaky's heart was racing. His brain was spinning fast at the moment. With this information, he had to find a way to make amends. And quickly.

"I've never been interested in a girl before, either. When I first saw her in the forest, our eyes met. Our bodies vibrated. We found it strange but nothing more. When we came here to the riverbank for the first time, the animals were all around us. It was like, magical. And there was a lightning bolt that passed between us. It was as if our bodies were finally reuniting. I know it may sound crazy to you, but I swear it's true. I felt like time stood still for a moment."

"I know, she told me about it."

"She told you? What did she say?"

"That she felt your soul touch hers. She also felt like she was meeting someone familiar. As if her body recognized yours."

"Wow. We might be soulmates. I have to go talk to her. It can't wait."

"No," Isabelle said firmly. "Give her time. She needs to see all of this for herself. She must realize that even though she's Stella's daughter, it doesn't change who she is. She needs to move forward and come to us. Otherwise, her journey of acceptance will never progress."

"You're right. You're very wise and mature for your age."

"That's true; I think it comes from my parents. They were very responsible and devoted people. And my adoptive parents taught me to make decisions and take on responsibilities at a very young age."

They stood there with their feet in the water for a good while. Inaky explained to her what their school year would look like at this college. Even though Inaky was fairly new, he had been part of this big family forever. His elementary school was nothing like the girls' elementary school. Already, he was learning to control his power. Neither was high school. He had a similar foundation, writing French and mathematics, but in a different way. He was learning to make ointments to heal a scrape he could get from falling off his bike, using plants found all over the forest. So, he had great knowledge and a good idea of what would await them in the next three years.

Lilou was lying on her stomach in her bed. Headphones were on her ears, and the music was fairly loud. She was flipping through a fashion magazine. Someone knocked on her door, but she didn't hear it. She saw the door open slowly. She took off her headphones and stretched her neck to see who was there.

"Hey beautiful, have you seen Isabelle? We haven't seen her since you got back from school."

"She went for a walk in the forest."

"But it's 5 o'clock, and she's still not back. Would you mind going to look for her, please?"

"Yes, okay, I'll go. It'll be good for me to get some fresh air."

Lilou put her headphones back on and went to look for Isabelle. She looked down as she walked. The ground was like a kind of earth composted by all the leaves that fell every autumn and remained there. Beautiful flowers managed to grow despite the little sunlight that filtered through all the branches filled with dark green foliage.

'La Minette is tiny but very pretty and sweet in taste. The Cyclamen of Naples is a beautiful little purple flower that looks like butterflies. Le compagnon blanc is absolutely marvelous, and the white hydrangea twines around trees and forms like a pretty white dress around the bark.' As I approached the water, I felt a vibration in my stomach. I stopped for a moment and turned off my music. I recognized Isabelle's voice talking with someone. I approached slowly, and at that moment, Inaky straightened up and turned to face me.

"I felt your arrival," he said, embarrassed.

"Yes, I know. Isabelle, the parents would like you to come in, but it's supper time, and they are worried about you. They sent me to fetch you."

"Okay, thanks. I'm coming. Inaky explained what we must do this year at school and what we must learn. It's going to be great, you know."

"Yes, probably. Come on. We have to go in." I turned to leave.

Inaky thought he absolutely had to tell her something, but what? Come on, old boy, think of something, anything. He looked at Isabelle, hoping she would understand his dilemma. She gave him an encouraging nod, pushing him towards Lilou so he could talk to her.

"Lilou, I would like to apologize for today sincerely. I should never have said what I said to Evan. But for me, you are Lilou. Stella's daughter, yes, but Lilou above all. It's just that Stella is our Queen, and she is very important to us. You will be our next Queen. That's no a small thing. People will soon realize who you are without even wanting it."

"Why, what do you mean?"

"Because you come from the Royal family. You will have gifts unlike others, and everything is known in this school anyway."

"What do you mean by that?"

"Someone always can't keep their mouth shut, like at the office, and then others will repeat what they're told, and so on. By the end of the week, everyone will know who you are, and it's not because I told Evan... And the bus stops right in front of the estate. Everyone knows who's been living here for generations."

...a brief pause...

"You have to forgive me and remain my friend. Please."

"Why? Why should I trust you? How do I know you're not lying and won't repeat what I confide in you to everyone?"

"Because I'm telling you."

"That's not enough for me. Now, excuse me, but I have to go home. Isabelle can stay here if she wants, but I'm going back." I was leaving in a hurry. I was almost running. I didn't want Inaky to hold me back and flinch in front of his beautiful eyes. I needed time to think, but most importantly, I wanted him to think a bit longer.

"I honestly believe she'll never forgive me. She's really mad at me."

"Oh no, you don't understand girls, do you? She just wants to make you wait a bit. To make you believe she's not interested. So that you beg her for forgiveness, so you will be nice to her next time. That you've won her over."

"Wow. Girls are complicated!" He said, rolling his eyes and sitting back on the rock.

"Yes, but when you've won her over, and she forgives you, you'll be madly in love. And you'll thank me."

"What should I do then?"

"Tomorrow, bring her favorite candies. She loves gummy bears or raspberry gummies. Just tell her it's a gift to apologize."

"And will it work?"

"Maybe you'll have to start over two or three times, but she'll be flattered by the gesture and the effort you put in to make amends."

"Okay, so we'll meet tomorrow then." Inaky grabbed his shoes and ran off home in the opposite direction of Isabelle. She went to meet Lilou, and they didn't talk about Inaky during the journey back home.

They had their meal outside on the terrace. The evening was so gentle. There was no wind, not too much humidity, and not a single mosquito. There were grapes and apples on the table, and Lilou cut them into small pieces. The grapes are in half, birds are fighting to get them, and the apples are in small quarters that squirrels adore.

"I understand better now why mosquitoes don't bother us in your presence."

"What do you mean?"

"You're part of the Royal family of the forest. Mosquitoes respect you and don't come near you."

"Oh, come on, you're just talking nonsense."

"Oh really! Have you ever been bitten by a mosquito? Have you ever been afraid of getting stung by a wasp or a bee? Have you ever seen them up close?"

"Sure, I don't remember, but mosquitoes don't respect me. You're talking nonsense, Isabelle."

"She's right, my little wildflower. Insects, birds, or animals on this earth know who you are. A skunk will never spray you with its precious scent, nor will a bee sting you with its lone sting. The forest inhabitants behind us know who you are and will protect you as best they can."

"That's nonsense," she exclaimed. She pushed her chair forcefully, stood up, and stormed off to her room.

"Leave her be. It's a normal phase of acceptance," Stella said calmly.

"She's even more stubborn than I was and even more than you, Stella," Maminou said with a smile, winking at Isabelle.

Lilou's night was tumultuous. She had all sorts of nightmares. The trees entangled her with huge branches, and the animals all wanted to touch her. The birds wanted one of her hairs as a lucky charm in their nests. They all wanted to smell her scent. She smelled like flowers and small fruits. She screamed, "Let me go, let me go. Please, let me go." She was desperate, scared, and crying. She heard her name. Through the branches, she heard her name again and again. Inaky was there in the distance, but he couldn't come to her aid. He yelled, "You've taken away my right to approach you, so I can't come to help you." Her name was being called from afar.

"Liliane. Liliane, wake up. Wake up, my dear, it's just a nightmare," she opened her tear-soaked eyes and saw Stella leaning over her.

"Mom. Mom, I was so scared. The trees were trying to grab me and keep me prisoner, and the birds wanted to tear out my hair. I was so scared."

"I know, but you have nothing to fear. You are safe. It was just a nightmare. It's the sleep of acceptance. You're afraid to accept who you are, so your dreams scare you. I swear no one wants to harm you. On the contrary, everyone loves you, and you have an even greater strength than mine." Stella was overjoyed that she called her mom but pretended as if nothing had happened not to break the moment. She had her daughter nestled in her arms for the first time in 10 years, maybe even more. Stella breathed in the sweet scent of wildflowers, and memories of her as a baby, while she rocked her to sleep, came back slowly.

"Really? How do you know that?" Lilou twirled a strand of Stella's hair between her fingers.

"Because when you walk, the trees vibrate at your passage. The flowers rise to gaze upon you, and the birds follow out of curiosity. The forest has never been greener than it is now. Flowers are blooming behind the house that we haven't seen in years. Ask Mr. Henry. His roses are more beautiful than ever this season."

"Do you truly believe I possess such great power?" she asked, her voice tinged with uncertainty. "And that I will one day replace you?"

"It is your destiny to replace me one day," She replied solemnly. "And I believe you will be the greatest Queen we have ever known."

"Why did you never come to see me before? Why now and not earlier?" she inquired, searching his eyes for answers.

"To protect you. To protect all of you," She explained. "If Hades had known where to find you, he would have done everything to harm you and me. He knows that if he attacked you, I would come to your aid immediately. He would have used that opportunity to unleash a horrible war."

"But what does Hades truly want?" she pressed, her brow furrowed in confusion.

"He wants to own the earth. To take everything upon it,"

she answered frankly. "He wants to destroy everything that is a color or a scent because, for him, everything is black or gray. He would want every animal to serve him. To turn humans into slaves of hell and reign stronger than paradise."

"But why? Why does he want to destroy us so much? What have we done to make him hate us that much?" Lilou questioned, her voice trembling with a mixture of fear and disbelief.

"We forbade him from coming to earth because every time he did, he destroyed everything around him and killed innocent people. Simply because he didn't like them," she revealed with a heavy heart.

"Goddess, it's dreadful. How do you manage to keep him from getting out? Where is the place where he can cross between the two worlds?" asked Lilou, her eyes widening with worry.

"Behind the school. It's far from the school, don't worry. But the school is the best barrier because he despises children. You are like poison to him," concluded Stella in a calm tone. She didn't want to worry her.

"And also, since you all have a cat with you, he can't fool their noses. We don't know the exact location of the door from which he can come out, but we know it's somewhere behind the school."

"That's why there are so many cats everywhere in the school and on the campus. They are sort of our protectors."

"Yes, exactly. If someone approaches the door of hell, the cats sense it like a vibration, even from several kilometers away. They have several gifts, you know." She gently caressed her daughter's face. "They are our alarm system for all of us. Our protection."

"Now go back to sleep. You have school tomorrow, and you need all your energy to learn lots of things."

"You won't leave us ever again, will you?" Stella turned in the doorway before leaving the room.

"No, I'm never leaving again, now that you're old enough to understand and soon to defend yourself if needed. I have no reason to leave you. Good night."

"Good night... Mom."

For the rest of the night, Lilou slept very well. The morning was a bit tough, but nothing that a good glass of milk and a peanut butter toast couldn't fix after a hot shower. Stella had tears in her eyes when she left her room last night. She called her mom and didn't want her to leave again. She was very happy about it.

The arrival of the bus stressed me out a bit. I was going to have to talk to Inaky and Evan, and I didn't feel like it at all. I really felt like I had butterflies in my stomach. I kept telling myself, calm down. The big yellow bus stopped in front of me. The driver opened the big door to let Isabelle and me in. I took a deep breath and climbed the four steps one by one. Suddenly, those four steps felt like a huge staircase. I looked up for a moment, and Inaky looked at me with a pleading look for forgiveness. I took a seat on a free bench in the front, second row, without thinking about his beautiful yellow eyes, which I love so much. I knew I wouldn't be able to hold on for long. I wanted to be near him so badly, but at the same time, I wanted him to understand that what he had done had greatly disappointed me. Isabelle stood frozen for a moment between the two rows of seats. She glanced at the boys and shrugged her shoulders in a sign of helplessness. When we arrived at the college, I quickly got off and rushed straight into the crowd of students, heading quickly towards the girls' restroom. I didn't want to run into Inaky. I wasn't ready to forgive him and trust him again.

"Hey, what are you doing, Liliane? Why did you run like that? There's no rush!"

"I don't want to see Inaky, and I don't want him to apologize again because I don't forgive him. Not yet. And don't call me Liliane; I hate that!"

"Okay. Come on, we have to go to the locker to get our textbooks. Classes start in five minutes."

Friday, the day and the first week of school are almost over. Isabelle's parents are coming for the weekend to see their daughter. She's really looking forward to seeing her parents. Even though she's very happy to be here with us, she still misses them a lot. Her life has changed a lot in a very short time. Besides slowly entering the adult world with puberty, she changed cities, houses, schools, and lifestyles without her parents. It's a lot of things for both of us in a few weeks. A hand taps my shoulder as we head towards the bus to go home. I turned around abruptly. I took a deep breath to stay calm. I immediately knew it was Inaky, just by his scent.

"Hi. I have a little surprise for you. I thought you'd be happy." Inaky held a bag of candy in his hand. Isabelle was silently signaling him to leave. She was shifting her eyes from right to left while nodding her head at the same time. She was thinking to herself, "Come on, go away now. I told you: give her the candy and leave." Inaky looked at Isabelle, understood her look, and tried to read her thoughts, but it was impossible. He instinctively understood, handed the bag of candy to Lilou, and left.

"Well, have a good weekend, girls. See you Monday." He waved and walked to the back of the bus with Evan.

The beginning of the weekend was very pleasant with Isabelle's parents' visit. It would be too short, much too short in their minds. They took Friday and Monday off because it was a long drive for just a weekend. They were already there when we arrived after school. Isabelle recognized her father's car in the driveway. She jumped off the bus quickly, dropped her bag, and ran to hug her father, who was waiting in front of the big door. I picked up the backpack and ran to greet them. Since we are the last ones to get on the bus in the morning, you've probably guessed that we're the first to get off at the end of the day. The students looked down the driveway or tried to see what was happening at my place. But with the numerous huge trees that formed the driveway, we couldn't see anything at all, and that was the point.

On Sunday evening, after dinner, I went for a walk in the forest. I wanted to leave Isabelle alone with her parents for a bit. The weekend was already over; they would leave the next day after we left on the bus for school. I had my little bag of jujube bear candies of all colors. That's what Inaky had given me on Friday before I got on the bus. I love these little candies. I even crave them. The birds were all singing in chorus. I took deep breaths; the forest smelled so good. It's the sweetest scent in the world, a mix of flowers, tree sap, and damp foliage. I walked to the clearing and took off my sandals to soak my feet. The water was so cool, and the sun was bright and warm. I walked in the water, and the fish came to caress my legs. I had brought breadcrumbs and scattered them for the fish. The bigger ones did little spins of thanks for me. Butterflies came to rest on the flowers at the water's edge. Birds, squirrels, and all the little forest creatures gathered around to watch me. At that moment, I became aware of who I was. I watched a titmouse and a finch in the tree and asked them to come to my hand.

"Come on, if I am truly your future Queen, we must get to know each other and trust each other. Come to my hand. Come, don't be afraid. I'm as scared as you are; it's new for me to be able to talk to you, too. Come, I have bread in the palm of my hand. Come get it."

The titmouse landed on my hand and looked at me. I felt like the little bird was nodding at me. It flew off with a piece of bread in its beak. The finch did the same thing.

"They thank you and say that you will be the greatest Queen we've ever known," said a feminine voice behind me. I turned around in surprise. A girl about my age, with long light brown hair and blue eyes like a cloudless sky, stood behind me.

"Hi, I'm Eva. We have classes together. I come here often, too. It's the only place where I feel at peace and free."

"Hi, I'm..."

"Liliane. I know everyone at school talks about you, my dear. Stella's daughter is here this year. You have a reputation that precedes you, you know."

"Firstly, I hate being called Liliane," I said calmly. "Secondly, I am the daughter of a mother and a father. Thirdly, I hate above all being compared to my mother, whom I don't even know," I said suddenly, red with anger.

"Wow! I'm sorry. Truly sorry. I'm just telling you what they say about you at school. Personally, I believe that everyone has to prove themselves. Regardless of who our parents are, we start from the same point. We're both in the first year of college with little to no experience of the magic we can do, produce, or inflict."

"I agree with you. Sorry, it's just that I hate being seen only as Stella's daughter and not as myself. My name is Lilou," I said, extending my hand to her.

"Pleased to meet you, Lilou. I'm Eva, and I live on the other side of the forest, close to Inaky. He talks about you all the time, too," she replied.

"...How do you know what they're saying?" I gestured towards the animals, wanting to change the subject.

"I can hear them and talk back. They understand everything we say. Animals have the ability to understand any language. But not everyone can speak to them in return," Eva explained.

"Wow, that's really an amazing gift. So, they did tell you I would be a good Queen?"

"The best. They say they trust you but weren't sure if you were ready," Eva responded.

"Ready for what?"

"To accept them and to accept yourself. They sense your discomfort and inner questioning," she replied.

"I'm afraid of what's ahead, and at the same time, I don't know what to expect. I'm afraid of not being good enough, being a terrible Queen, and being unable to replace Stella. I'm so scared. I'm afraid of being ridiculed because I'm expected to be extraordinary compared to who I am. But if I don't have powers or can't control them or... I don't know what. But I'm so scared. I have a huge knot in my stomach," I confessed.

"We all have fears, you know. Not for the same reasons, because we won't have to protect the entire forest, but we don't know what our role will be in the future. Why can I talk to animals? How will it serve me in my life?" Eva shared.

"I really don't know. Do you want a jelly bear?" I presented her with the bag of gummy bears, and Eva took a few.

"The butterflies are asking if you're ready to see something. They want to show you a side of their personality you've never seen before."

"Yes, yes, I'm ready. I must understand that I don't live in the world I thought I did, but in an extraordinary world."

The butterflies approached her all together. There were plenty of them, maybe fifty. In all colors, it was magical. They made a banner, and the closer they got, the more she perceived something amazing. The butterflies were...

"It's unbelievable. You're miniature humans with wings! I must be dreaming; this can't be possible."

"Yes, it's possible. Normal humans don't see us because they don't take the time to see us. They see us, but they don't observe us like you do." A small voice replied.

"I can hear you, and I hear you talking to me. Eva, I heard them."

"You've never heard them before?"

"No."

Eva turned to the animals and questioned them all. They discussed for a while among themselves. But I watched in silence because Eva was talking to them telepathically.

"They say that no apprentice Queen has ever heard them before. Queens usually have a translator. And they only communicate, like me, through telepathy. Can you really hear them talking?"

"Like I hear you."

"It's unbelievable. The fish say it happened once, a very long time ago."

"In the 1800s, the Queen spoke to the fish. She had assembled an army of whales to sink pirate ships attempting to enter our world. It was Hades who had seized the ships, killing everyone on board. She had disguised herself as a mermaid while leaning on a whale's nose and had ordered the ships to leave her waters. Hades had tried to kill her, and she had commanded the whales to take those ships into the deepest waters. Since Hades couldn't withstand the water, he returned to hell with his entire crew."

"What a story. Do Queens usually have a translator?"

"Yes, there has never been another Queen before you who could speak and understand animals. Except for this one I'm telling you about, but that was so long ago."

"So, what if we keep this secret between us, and you become my translator? I think it might be good if no one knows about my gift right away. What do you think?"

"I agree. Maybe one day we'll know if we can reveal it or if we had the brilliant idea not to tell anyone."

"Well, now we know what your gift is for," Lilou said, nudging her friend playfully.

"What are you not telling anyone?" asked a male voice behind us.

"You scared us, Inaky," Eva said. "We jumped and scared the fish."

"I'm sorry. I thought you heard me coming."

"No, we didn't hear you coming. Please announce yourself next time," I replied.

"Besides being transparent, Inaky, you're not very loud."

"Sorry. So, what won't you tell anyone?"

"Anyone, Inaky. Anyone, including you. Bye, Eva, I'm going home. See you tomorrow at school."

"Okay, bye, see you on the bus," I didn't even greet Inaky. I paused for a moment and turned around.

"Thanks for the candies. But that doesn't excuse you. Not yet, anyway."

"Okay," Inaky replied with a nod of understanding.

"What did you do this time, Inaky?" Eva asked, looking discouraged.

"On the first day of school, I revealed her secret and told Evan who she really was. I mean, who she really is. And now she thinks it's my fault that everyone at school knows."

"But it was the cats who spread the rumor."

"I know, but she doesn't know that, and she won't listen to me, so she thinks I broke our trust."

"But you have to tell her and apologize."

"I did, even several times. But she doesn't believe me."

"Okay. Tomorrow, when we get to school, I'll take her to the little park behind the school. Be there, and I'll ask the cat masters to tell her the truth, and then she'll forgive you."

"Do you think it will work?"

"I think so. At least we have nothing to lose by trying."

Isabelle found it very difficult to leave for school Monday morning because her parents were leaving for home at the same time.

"We're trying to find work around here. We'll miss you, sweetheart, and the house is for sale. We'll come and settle here as soon as we can."

"I'll miss you too. We'll see each other next month, right?"

"Yes, my princess," said her father, "I'm looking for a job here. And your mother will find out if she could be transferred to a school here," her father replied, holding back his tears.

"You know, I love being here," Isabelle replied, "I really like school and being with Lilou. But I miss you both a lot. Our mealtime conversations and game nights are missed. I hope you'll come soon. In the meantime, shall we talk on Skype in the evenings?"

"Yes, my dear, we talk every evening," her mother said. "And we're doing everything possible to come here as soon as possible." Her mother hugged her tightly and showered her with kisses. Her father held her in his arms and whispered in her ear.

"Take good care of yourself, my dear, and look after Lilou. Be careful with boys."

"Yes, Dad, don't worry. I love you too."

"Your bus is here, and you'll be late for school."

They hugged tightly, and Isabelle got on the bus with red eyes. Lilou waved goodbye to Isabelle's parents and remained silent during the journey. She arrived at school and saw Eva at the main gate, watching for their arrival. She waved to her through the window.

"I have a new friend to introduce to you," I told Isabelle as we got off the bus. "She's super nice, and you know what? She talks to animals."

"To animals?"

"Yes, any animal. She hears them talk, and she responds to them telepathically."

"Wow, what an incredible gift." Eva took me by the arm as we walked back.

"Come here. I want to show you something at the back of the school."

"Wait, I want to introduce you to a friend of mine. Eva, meet Isabelle, she's like a sister."

"Hi, come with us. I have to show you something."

"Okay. But how come you're already here?"

"I asked my father to drop me off earlier; I needed to prepare something."

"Wha....what have you done, Eva? I was worried. Had she gathered everyone to announce who I really was?"

"Don't worry, I have something important to show you. Or rather, someone to introduce you to."

Arriving at the back of the school, I saw a huge gray, white, and orange cat. It was as big as a raccoon. Maybe even bigger.

"Lord, is this really a cat?"

"Show some respect, please. I am the master cat. I know you are the future Queen, my dear," the cat replied with disarming coldness.

"The cat asks for a little respect because she is the master cat. She's a bit like the Queen, too. And she says she knows you are the future Queen."

"Okay. I'm sorry, I didn't mean to disrespect you."

"How come I can understand what she's saying?" She looked at Lilou and Eva in turn.

"She can understand you too, but she wants to keep this secret for as long as possible," Eva replied in her mind.

"My grandfather told me about a mermaid who spoke to fish and animals, but I didn't believe it since no Queen spoke an animal language after that. Don't worry. I'll keep the secret. What can I do for you?"

I was waiting for Eva to speak since I had to act as if I heard nothing but cat meows. At that moment, Inaky arrived, followed by his friend Evan.

"What's he doing here?" I asked Eva.

"I asked him to come because I want to make you understand something. Let me talk to Ziny, and you'll understand," Eva replied.

"Ziny? Who's that?" I inquired.

"The cat. Her name is Ziny. Give me a minute. I know you can hear her response, so I can't make things up. I want you to hear it for yourself," Eva explained. She then asked Ziny, "Who spread the rumor about Stella's daughter arriving?"

"It was me," Ziny admitted.

"Because Lilou is convinced it's Inaky since he told Evan once. But now that the whole school knows, she's sure Inaky broke the secret and betrayed her trust," Eva elaborated.

"All right, say it out loud so everyone knows the truth. Lovers will be able to kiss, and everyone can be happy," suggested Ziny.

Inaky, Isabelle, Evan, and I watched Eva and the big cat. We wondered what they could be talking about. I almost responded to Ziny that we weren't lovers. I shouldn't reveal that I understand cat language. I remained silent.

"It was she who spread the news of your arrival. Not Inaky. He only told Evan and no one else. You have to forgive him and accept his apologies," Eva concluded.

"You brought me here for this? But why did the cat tell everyone? And it's a girl?" I questioned.

"Because everyone was waiting for your arrival. And yes, Ziny is the mother queen of all cats."

"Why? Why was everyone waiting for my arrival?" I asked.

"Because you're Stella's daughter. You're like a princess or a star or something, but the whole school was eagerly awaiting your arrival," Isabelle replied.

"But I'm not a princess, certainly not a star. I'm just Lilou. Lilou, who knows nothing about this world and has no power," I protested.

"You have powers. You might not know them yet, but you do have them," Isabelle reassured her.

"Maybe, but I want to be seen for Lilou and not as Stella's daughter and have an indescribable pressure on my shoulders," I insisted.

"We understand that, but not everyone will think like that. It will be up to you to set them straight," Isabelle said, taking her hand. "Now we have to go in because we'll be punished if we're late. It'll be a great way for you to get noticed."

"I don't want to be noticed. Let's go," Lilou said, ready to enter.

"Wait," Inaky said, gently grabbing her arm. "Can you forgive me now, and we'll be friends again?"

"We'll talk about that later. We have to get in right now. The bell just rang for the second time, which means we have only 5 minutes before the doors close," Lilou replied, hurrying inside.

"Okay, see you at the clearing after school," Inaky said.

"All right." Lilou turned around and thanked Ziny for keeping the secret with a glance and a nod. The cat understood and did the same.

The day crawled by slowly. Isabelle, Eva, and I went to have our lunch outside in the park. The weather was so nice. The sun was shining brightly, and it felt like the warmth of July at the end of September. Birds were circling above us. Squirrels were eagerly waiting for us to leave so they could gather the crumbs on the ground. A butterfly landed on my shoulder and whispered something in my ear.

"Then I took a piece of my grapes and placed it on my shoulder," Eva watched Isabelle's reaction intently, having heard the butterfly's request to me. But I hadn't thought about Isabelle.

"Why are you putting a piece of grape on your shoulder, and how can a butterfly land on your shoulder like that? I've never seen a butterfly come so close to a person," Isabelle exclaimed, her curiosity piqued. I glanced at Eva, realizing I hadn't anticipated Isabelle noticing.

"Well... I have to tell you a secret that Eva and I discovered yesterday," I began cautiously, aware of Isabelle's keen interest in our conversation. She looked back and forth between Eva and me, her expression asking, "What are you about to tell me?"

"You absolutely must keep this secret and not tell anyone," I emphasized, stressing the importance of confidentiality.

"Okay, no problem. You know you can trust me," Isabelle assured me, leaning in slightly to hear better.

I scanned our surroundings, making sure no one else would overhear what I was about to reveal to Isabelle.

"I can understand the language of animals," I confessed, waiting for Isabelle's reaction. She remained composed, absorbing this revelation.

"I don't understand. What do you mean by understanding animals?" Isabelle inquired, her curiosity growing.

"I can communicate with them. They speak to me, and I respond. I understand them as I understand you. It's like we're speaking the same language," I explained, trying to articulate the unique bond I shared with animals.

"But isn't that Eva's gift?" Isabelle questioned, recalling Eva's abilities.

"Yes, but I can do it too," I affirmed, eager to share this aspect of myself with Isabelle.

"There was only one Queen in the past who had this gift. She could also transform into a mermaid and communicate with whales, it was back in the 1800s. Several people, like me, communicate with animals through telepathy. However, not a Queen, let alone an apprentice," Eva chimed in, providing historical context to my revelation.

"Lilou can truly speak the language of animals. They converse while I communicate through thoughts," Eva added, clarifying her own abilities in contrast to mine.

"You will be an extraordinary Queen, Lilou. You will rewrite history. I am certain you will discover many other powers within yourself. Wow, what did the butterfly say to you?" Isabelle felt proud deep down to be the best friend of a future incredible Queen. She is proud of her bestie.

"She asked if she could have a piece of grape. It's been a long time since she had one."

"Is it a girl?"

"Yes, it's a girl. Butterflies are only females; the males are the bumblebees."

"Wow, I didn't know insects had sexes to that extent. Talking to animals must be cool; you both are lucky. I don't have any powers."

"But of course, you have one. Come on. We just haven't discovered it yet. Give yourself some time," Lilou told her, hoping she was right.

"Time, we are surrounded by extraordinary young ones, and some here have discovered their gift even before they could walk. So if I had a gift, I would have known before today."

"Hey, I discovered that I could talk to animals just last night and make a flower grow back at the beginning of summer. I didn't even know until this year that I was a... a... I don't even know what to call it."

"I was eight years old when I heard my dog Sally say she hated her kibble to my mother."

"And what did you do?"

"I told my mother, 'Sally doesn't like this food; it cramps her stomach.' And my mother asked me how I knew that. And I said, 'Because she tells you every time you give it to her again.'"

"And what did she say?" Isabelle asked.

"Since when do you talk to animals? My mother said."

"And I replied, since now, mom."

"What did she do?"

"She told me to tell Sally that she buys this food because it was cheaper, but since it makes her sick, she'll change it as soon as the bag is empty!"

"What did you do?"

"I told Sally to look even sicker so that mom would change the bag as soon as possible. The next day, my mom took the rest of the big bag to the nearest shelter as a donation."

"You're awesome."

"Yes, and Sally thanked me every day after that."

"Is she still alive?"

"Yes, she's old now, but still in good shape. She's nine years old and still runs with me in the forest. She loves it."

"Oh, the bell. We have to finish this school day. Leave your bread crusts, Isabelle. The birds and squirrels are waiting for them."

The three of us got on the bus in the afternoon, and I sat in the front again. I avoided looking at Inaky when he got on. I wanted to wait at the clearing to talk to him, hoping we would be alone. How do I tell him that I'm sorry? Sorry for thinking he was the one who told everyone who I really was. How do I tell him that I trust him and that I missed him terribly the past week? Without seeming desperate.

I don't know how to tell Inaky that I really like him without starting to act like an idiot. I'm crazy about him. I would like him to be my first kiss. I don't want him to think I'm drooling over him and that he can do whatever he wants with me. I want him to respect me as I respect him. I don't know how it's done. Yes, I know this is my second kiss. But does that one with Nathan really count? Okay, fine, my second kiss. Except for this one, I sincerely hope there will be a second and a third.

The questions kept swirling in my mind. 'Who could I ask all these questions to?' No one in my circle would answer all these questions without asking, 'Who are you talking about?' Ah, maybe one person. As I got off the bus, I told Isabelle we would meet later because I needed to talk to Mr. Henry and then go to the clearing to speak with Inaky.

"Okay, don't worry, I won't disturb you, even though I'd love to turn into a little mouse and hear and see this meeting."

"Why? Nothing extraordinary will happen. I'll just tell him that I accept his apologies and apologize for unfairly accusing him. That's it."

"Really? Do you really think I'll believe that? You two are made for each other, and everyone knows it. It's palpable when you're near each other. You can feel it in the air when you're so close to each other."

"What are you talking about?"

"You're in love with him, and he's crazy in love with you. There are sparks or static in the air when you're close. Don't tell me otherwise. Eva and I noticed it when we were at the park to meet the big cat."

"Ziny the cat."

"Yes, Ziny the cat. Even though I noticed it all summer, I became aware of it with Eva. I don't know exactly what she saw, but I felt like an electric wire was trying to tie you two together."

"Do you remember when you caught us just as we were about to kiss?"

"Yes."

"Well, we felt an electric current run through our bodies when our hands touched. It was like we were connecting to each other. Like our bodies were reuniting with someone they had lost long ago."

"Yes, as you explained to me the other day. Do you believe that you are soul mates?" Isabelle said excitedly at the idea.

"I don't know. Is it possible? Anyway, I don't even know what to say to him."

"Tell him what you feel. Tell him that you apologize and that you accept his apologies. That's all."

"It's not that simple. I'm afraid of stuttering and saying something silly in front of him. I'm afraid of looking like a real fool. I've never really talked to a boy before."

"Me neither. I've never kissed anyone either."

"Yes, you kissed Paul 3 or 4 years ago during the bottle game." Lilou reminded her with a little smile.

"That doesn't count. He did it on purpose. I mean a real kiss."

"Me neither."

"Yes, you kissed Nathan. Remember? The beautiful Nathan."

"Yes, that's true, Nathan, and he kissed really well. It's a bit embarrassing for me. What if I kiss badly, and he never wants to kiss me again?"

"Well, no, come on. I think you'll kiss each other really well and for a long time. A long, languorous, and delicious kiss," Isabelle said, dancing a kind of waltz. "Ha ha ha!" She giggled.

"Stop it, you're embarrassing me. Anyway, we'll catch up later. I have to talk to Mr. Henry. And brush my teeth just in case."

"Yes, okay, you'll tell me everything. I want to know everything."

I walked along the forest path leading to the clearing and thought about what Mr. Henry had told me.

"Listen to your heart. It will guide you," I murmured to myself. "Tell him everything you feel. Look into his eyes; he will see your feelings. You don't have to be afraid; he loves you too. Then he will understand what you mean." Mr. Henry advised me earlier when I went to talk to him.

'How do you simply tell a boy you love him, 'I love you'?' My hands were clammy as I reached the water's edge. No one was around. My stomach twisted inside me. Shoes off, pants rolled up to my knees, I listened to all the sounds with my eyes closed. I took deep breaths. "Breathe, breathe," my conscience whispered. "Take deep breaths." Did I have good breath? Oh, Lord, my legs were trembling.

'It smells so good here,' I thought, the scent of late summer flowers mingling with the damp grass and the water, still strangely warm. Everything smelled good to me. I could hear every sound of the forest as if in a dream. A squirrel was eating a nut. A bird was fortifying its nest for the approaching winter. Bees were gathering the last pollen before hibernation. I felt the moisture in the air on my arms and face. A profound sense of well-being washed over me like a sudden burst of energy.

Opening my eyes, I saw Inaky standing before me. 'Goddess, he's beautiful,' I thought. His short, curly, dark hair like ebony. His bright yellow eyes shine, and his candy-pink lips taste like raspberries.

"I didn't hear you come," I said softly.

"You looked so peaceful. I didn't want to disturb or scare you. Nature loves you, you know," Inaky replied. "Look around you. The trees persist in staying green in your presence, and the flowers still produce pollen in late September. I've never seen this forest so beautiful in my life. Look at all the fish around you. They feed on your energy."

"And I absorb their energy. I feel so good here. I really feel like I'm at home," I replied, a memory of Mr. Henry's words echoing in my mind. "You're at home here. You can never get lost in the forest; it's your home," he had said, and he was right.

A little silence. Looks. They took a deep breath and closed their eyes for a moment.

"I owe you an apology. Please allow me to express myself first, and then you can share your thoughts." I had set a goal for myself to begin. Even if I stumble along the way, I'll pick myself up and start again. There's only one way to say it! "I regret accusing you of revealing my true self to everyone. I'm sorry for not listening to you or trusting you when you assured me it wasn't your fault and that you would never betray our mutual trust. I apologize for not treating you kindly. I hope you can forgive me in return." After a brief pause, Inaky waited to see if I had finished. "I've missed you a lot. I enjoy your company immensely. I feel comfortable when you are near. Your sense of humor brightens my day; I find you funny, and we never get bored with you. I would like us to take our relationship to the next level. I would like you to become my boyfriend."

Inaky says nothing. He remains silent. I am starting to get very nervous. But what is he saying to himself? If I could read his mind, I would know what foot to dance on.

"I will not tell you anything. I will show you." He draws me towards him with great gentleness. Puts an arm around my waist.

At that moment, without Lilou knowing it, they both become transparent. There is no question of anyone coming to disturb this moment he had been waiting for since the beginning of the summer. Lilou has butterflies in her stomach. Her legs have difficulty supporting her standing, and ants seem to be dancing the samba there. She trembles like a leaf in the wind. A kiss. He is going to give her, her first kiss. She places one hand on his neck and the other circled his muscular chest for a young man of 17 years old. Lilou feels like she has a winter storm in her stomach. They close their eyes, and their lips brush together. Inaky stops for a moment to see her reaction or to prolong this moment.

That perfect moment of anticipation is sometimes better than the kiss itself. You know that moment when you wonder what it will be like, sweet, pleasant, truly amazing. The moment when it feels like time stops, and it's just the two of you. May the whole universe be in suspense, waiting for this first warm, impatient contact. Their hot, rapid breaths cross each other. Inaky runs his other hand through her hair and takes possession of her mouth. Lilou feels like she is losing consciousness. Inaky's soft lips kiss hers as if they had known each other forever. Their tongues cross and uncover each other. She steadies herself and tightens her grip. The heat and their breathing increase by several degrees. The innocent hands discover their young forms and leave a trace of pleasure. The kiss lasts a very, very long time. The bruised lips and the lack of oxygen give reason to their thirst for kisses. Lilou buries her head in the crook of his neck and tightens her arms around Inaky. He takes a deep breath in Lilou's hair.

"You smell so good. You smell like a sylvester."

"My grandmother always calls me her little wildflower or my little Sylvester."

"It must be your lucky flower, then. Is your favorite color purple?"

"Yes, pink, pale purple, and turquoise. The color of a sylvan tree. Your eyes are so beautiful. I could watch them endlessly and still not get enough of them."

"You will be able to look at them your whole life. You are so beautiful, Lili. I'm glad you forgive me. I missed you a lot, too. Evan couldn't stand hearing me talk about you anymore. I think another week, and I would have lost him as a friend."

"Never again will I judge you before having spoken to you. I believe in you. I would like us to tell each other everything and never argue again. I like that you call me Lili."

"It feels different from the others. Only I have the right to call you Lili," he said. "I agree with you, my little flower. I never want us to argue again." Inaky leans in and gently kisses her lips. "Hmm! I love your lips."

"Great, because I love yours too," she replies. "I know you can read other people's thoughts, but I'd like you not to read mine. It wouldn't be fair because I can't know what you're thinking."

"I would never do that. And I don't constantly read people's thoughts. Only when it's necessary. Or when I need to know a score or for a laugh. But never to my friends."

"Why is that owl already up and won't stop screaming?"

"Because it's my brother who wants me to come home. And he's looking for me."

"Your brother!"

"Yes, my younger brother. And my parents can turn into owls, too. I am transparent and can read thoughts. And my youngest sister can change her hair color or take any animal form."

"Wow, you have an interesting family. It must be great to be a cat or a bird to spy on people all day."

"Maybe, but being transparent has its advantages, too," he says, capturing her lips in one last kiss before reappearing. "Hmm, what a kiss." Chills ran through Lilou's body, making her wonder if the temperature had suddenly changed. "I love you, Lili." 'Always have,' he thinks to himself.

"I love you too, Inaky."

"I have to go. I have a potion to prepare for tomorrow morning."

"I should go inside, too. It must be nearly dinnertime."

One last kiss before parting. The two lovers go in opposite directions. They live at opposite ends of each other. Lilou has never been to the other side of the forest.

She doesn't even know what the village where Inaky and several of his friends live might look like," she thinks. 'I must visit this village one day. It can't be very different from here,' she tells herself on the way back. Isabelle is waiting for her on a lounge chair, enjoying the last rays of the sun for the day.

"How did it go?" Isabelle asks, very curious.

"Very well. We talked, and everything went very well. We forgave each other, and we are friends again."

"Is that all?" Isabelle retorted, certain that she was hiding something else.

"Yes, that's all. What more do you want?" Lilou was embarrassed to tell her about the first kiss. She still had the taste of plums in her mouth.

"I don't know, a kiss, maybe?"

"Oh, that! Yes, we kissed." Lilou said nothing more to keep Isabelle in suspense.

"AND... How was it? Tell me, I want to know everything."

They made themselves comfortable on the terrace, retrieving a cozy blanket from the storage box. As the evening air grew cooler, the sun slipped behind the dense forest of trees. Lilou told her everything, describing the tingling sensation that ran through her body. The feeling of weightlessness as they kissed. How she felt like she was floating and nothing existed around them anymore. They both dreamed of love, sitting on a deck chair wrapped in a fleece blanket and breathing in the scents of late summer. Lost in their own dream of love. They relaxed together, enveloped in the sweetness of the end of the day.

****

October settled in, and very soon, everything was colored. Orange, yellow, red, and all the color ranges mixed together formed a truly magnificent backdrop behind the house. With all these fantastic colors, Halloween and its pumpkins. The children who will pass by to collect as many candies as possible reminded us of all the preparations for the long winter season.

We need to chop wood for the many fireplaces in the house. Store the summer chairs, umbrellas, and everything that can't stay outside during the white season in the sheds.

Prepare the feeders for the birds and other animals that come to feed here. Grandma needs to gather all her spice gardens to preserve them during the winter for her potions, teas, potions, and ointments.

We also need to clear the entire vegetable garden and pick all the remaining fruits, apples, pears, ground cherries, and others to preserve them or dry them in the barn.

Remove the mosquito nets from the many windows so they don't rust. Check for leaks, tie up the bushes, and wrap them in a net to protect them from the wind. There were so many things to do, but Henry was super happy to have several people this year to help him. He would even have time for himself in the evening for once.

I was kneeling on the ground, placing wood in an antique chest for my fireplace in my room, when someone knocked on my window. I looked out the window but saw no one. I stood up, walked towards the window, and opened it. There was no one there.

"Let me in, it's me, Inaky. I am transparent, so no one sees me going to your room," a voice said.

"Come in, you scared the hell out of me! Don't do that again, please. You scare me when you talk, and I can't see you," she whispered in response. "I could never get used to it."

"Okay, I'll try to warn you before next time. It's just very convenient. I can come to say goodnight, and no one knows I'm here," Inaky replied.

"I know, but it scares me every time," she admitted.

"You'll get used to it," he said. He placed his hands on her waist and pulled her closer. His warm breath smelled of wild strawberries, and Lilou almost lost track of where she was. He closed his eyes and kissed her rosy lips. "Goodness! His skillful tongue made her lose all composure. Lilou wrapped her arms around his neck and kissed him softly. Gradually, a knot formed in her stomach, her legs felt weak, and she had stomach spasms.

"Lilou, have you finished stacking your wood?" The door opened gently. Lilou found herself alone, feeling off balance and breathing irregularly. Her thoughts were fuzzy, and her cheeks were as red as a tomato.

"Is everything okay, Lilou?" her grandmother asked.

"Uh! Yes, yes, everything's fine. I think I'm just exhausted. And you startled me."

"We worked hard today, it's normal. Have you finished stacking all your wood?"

"Yes." Lilou wondered if Inaky was still there and, if so, where he was. She dared not move to avoid stepping on his foot and risking exposure.

"I'm going to bed right now. I'll take a shower and then sleep."

"Well, see you tomorrow then. Good night." Grandmother closed the door but didn't leave right away. She was listening at the door.

"Inaky appeared at that moment. Lilou signaled him with her finger to stay silent and pointed to the door. She knew her grandmother was listening on the other side. She must have suspected something about the way she looked when she entered the room, as she was kissing her boyfriend. Lilou went to the bathroom, turned on the water, returned to the room, rummaged through her drawers to make noise, and took her pajamas. She heard her grandmother slowly moving away. The floors are so noisy that it's impossible to escape silently here. She returned to the bathroom with Inaky, closed the door behind her, and locked it."

"Phewed! We had a close call on that one," said Inaky.

"Yes, I was so dizzy, and my thoughts were all over the place because it happened so fast. We need to be careful never to get caught," replied Lilou.

"Yes, I'll be more cautious next time."

"What do you mean, 'next time'? You don't seriously intend to come here every night, do you?"

"Why not? I like coming here to wish you good night, hidden from viewers and sheltered from the cold."

"I don't think that's a good idea. It would be tempting fate unnecessarily."

"Why do you say that?"

"Because I'm not ready for anything other than tender kisses and caresses."

"Don't worry about that, neither am I. Your sweet kisses and scent are more than enough for me. I love being close to you, I love kissing you, but I know we're too young for sexual relations."

"That's good. At least things are clear, and we know where the boundaries are."

They looked into each other's eyes in silence. Lilou leaned in and kissed his enticing lips. Several minutes later, Lilou reluctantly let go of Inaky's embrace. "You have to leave; I need to shower and sleep. There won't be any hot water left if this keeps up."

"Okay, I'll go. Goodnight, see you tomorrow."

"Yes, see you tomorrow, sweet dreams." They walked towards the window, and Lilou took his hand. "Inaky, how can I know that you've really left? You could easily spy on me and watch me shower, and I would never know!"

"I will never do such a thing. I will never violate your personal space without asking for permission. I don't spy on people in their intimate or very personal moments. I can't do that. It would be shameful for my power."

"How could you know I wasn't naked before coming to knock on my window?"

"I asked for help from a bird."

"A bird!"

"Yes, I asked it to come and see at your window, and it told me you were placing wood in a bin and that you had clothes. And that you were alone, of course."

"Wow, I didn't know you could talk to animals."

"There are so many things you don't know about me, my dear Lili. I can't wait to teach you everything about my personality and secrets."

"You have secrets, you little rascal..." They kissed one last time, and Lilou quickly jumped into the shower before someone came to tell her to turn off the water.

She had many dreams that night. Sweet dreams with Inaky in the forest. She dreamed of her mother explaining how to make healing potions. Hades disturbed her sleep. He had no face. She couldn't be sure it was him since she didn't know what he looked like. His face was permanently shadowed or like a dark cloud. He tried to grab her with his large claws from hell and said,

"I will prevent you from destroying me. I will destroy you first. You will never be able to stop me from reigning. I will reign over your cursed land and eliminate all of you, down to the last man. Get ready because my army will be ready to face you very soon. In a few months, everything you know on this earth will end. The darkness of the shadows will be all that remains."

"Lilou, Lilou wake up!" A feminine voice called her in her dream.

Lilou jumped in her bed with a gasping breath. She breathed deeply to calm herself, glad to realize it was just a dream. She felt a presence in her room. Sleepy eyes and lack of light prevented her from seeing who was there. She stretched to turn on the light on the bedside table near her bed.

"What are you doing here?" Lilou asked.

"I wanted to see you, and I felt like you were having a nightmare. I came to see if you were okay." Her mother was sitting on Lilou's reading chair at the end of the bed.

"I'm fine. Was it you calling my name? I dreamt about Hades."

"Yes, to wake you up. Do you want to talk about it?"

"He was trying to grab me with his big claws. He told me to be ready because his army was almost ready to come and destroy everything I knew on earth. Every last man. I couldn't see his face but knew it was him."

"Goddess! Did he say anything else to you?"

"That he would kill me to reign over the earth. That I couldn't stop him from taking my place and destroying everything."

"...a long silence. Stella had chills down her spine."

"Mom, tell me it's just a dream. That he didn't really come to talk to me and that we won't be at war for real in a few months?"

"He said in a few months?"

"Yes. He said that I won't recognize anything I knew on earth in a few months, that only darkness will remain."

Her mother quickly got up from the chair and ran out of the room. "Follow me."

"Where are you going? Mom?" Lilou got out of bed, put on her rabbit-shaped slippers, and followed her mother into the hallway. "Mom, what's going on? Where are you going?"

"I'm going to wake up your father. We need to discuss this immediately."

Lilou took her arm firmly and made her turn to face her.

"Do tell me what's going on. It was just a dream, Mom."

"We don't dream of Hades. He comes to talk to us and traumatize us. You're barely initiated, and he's already invading your dreams. You must truly have immeasurable strength among us all. But above all, he must really fear you and want to attack immediately. He doesn't want us to have time to prepare and train you. Otherwise, you'll be too powerful for him. He's afraid. We need to accelerate your learning."

"What do you mean by accelerating my learning? Mom? Mom?" Lilou was almost running after her mother. "Answer me, please. You're scaring me."

"We need to wake your father first."

She woke everyone up and told them to go down to the main hall. Stella started the coffee maker and lit a fire in the large fireplace with a snap of her fingers. They would be up for a while, so it was better to warm up the room and wake everyone up well because important decisions had to be made that night. After serving coffee to everyone and taking a few sips herself, she began to explain Lilou's dream.

"We need to speed up the training process for the young ones this year. We need to prioritize combat and healing classes, combat weapon crafting, and drop all the others, or almost all."

"We can't drop potion and remedy making, weapon crafting teaching, shields, those for whom the teachers need replacements."

"That's true, but if Hades arrives with his army in a few weeks, we'll all be dead in a few days." Stella tried to keep calm. But the mere idea of losing her daughter because she wasn't prepared made her feel nauseous.

"We don't have enough students to craft, repair, heal, and attack."

"We need to find a solution. Starting tomorrow, we have to change our way of teaching and prepare them for battle," said Stella nervously.

Lilou and Isabelle were sitting next to each other, trembling with fear. Isabelle not only learned that she was part of their family and that she might have powers, but now, she had to learn to fight, heal, and cure. To eliminate Hell! She kept telling herself that this was all just a dream. That she would soon wake up in the stone house where she grew up. In her white canopy bed with her parents beside her, and that all this would be just a horrible nightmare.

"Lilou, pinch me, please. This must be a nightmare. None of this makes sense. We don't even know if I have power, I know nothing about your world, and you want me to learn to fight against the forces of hell. You're crazy," Isabelle exclaimed as she got up from the couch and ran out of the living room.

"I'll go talk to her. Find a solution before sunrise. We need to come to school with plans and answers to several questions that will be asked of us," said Adèle, leaving the room to join Isabelle.

"How many children do we have from first grade to senior year? And how many in college?" inquired Stella.

"With last year's graduates, who are in practical training this year. There were three graduation classes, with about 25 students each. There are three classes of 5th graders this year, with 20 students each. There are two classes of each grade from 1st to 4th, also with 20 students each," Stella calculated the number of students this year. "We have 295 students at school this year. Plus, there are over 300 students in college. It's hard to have the exact number."

"Over 300 children to send to war. It makes no sense. We can't sacrifice our children for our future. We're not numerous enough to fight hell," Louis stated.

"We must call upon all wizard parents and their families. Train the students for succession and support the adults. We must call upon everyone who wants to save the earth and close hell forever," concluded Lilou, very anxious.

Lilou had shivers all over her body as she said these words. She thought these shivers were nothing like the ones she had felt a few hours earlier when she kissed Inaky.

"You're right, Lilou. We shouldn't sacrifice our children but rather prepare them for the future. We all must participate in this war to end it once and for all. We must issue a call to everyone today. We must go into the forest to speak to the animals so they can pass the message on to others," suggested Albert.

"I know people who talk to animals, and I have friends who can transform. They can go farther and faster than us to deliver the message. I also know young people who live in the neighboring village; they can transmit it to other communities that could be useful to us," Lilou said. She was thinking about Inaky and couldn't stop saying his name in her head.

"I'll communicate with the parents, at least those I know, and I'll tell them to reach out to those they know," Louis said as he left the room with these final words. There was a knock on the front door. "I'll go see who it is," Louis said, leaving the room.

"I can also speak to the elders; we'll be very useful in training the young ones. You'll need teachers to teach them everything quickly. If there are several teachers, we could form small groups and be more present for each student. We would be more productive," Alfred, the guardian of the sacred water, suggested. He would have to train the next guardian of the water. He had always been a magnificent warrior and had an excellent sword. He remembered when he trained Louis for his weapon manipulation exam. Louis came to the top of the class and even received honors thanks to him. Louis had always thanked him for teaching him how to handle the sword. Alfred thought as Louis went to open the front door. "I could also take this opportunity to choose who will replace me as the guardian of the sacred water," Alfred said.

"You're right, Alfred. Many elders would make very good teachers. Ask Adèle to talk to her friends, too, for potions and remedies," Stella said. Adèle was trying to calm Isabelle, who was crying in her room.

It was 5:00 in the morning. The sun was starting to rise. Everyone got to work. Lilou got up to go to her room.

"Lilou, there's someone here for you," Louis pointed to the front door. He whispered in her ear as she passed by. "Don't you think having friends over is a bit early?"

"I didn't invite any friends at this hour, Dad," Lilou replied. She spotted Inaky in the doorway. "What are you doing here?"

"You called me," he said.

"No, I didn't call you," Lilou insisted. Louis, hidden, listened in as a spy.

"Yes, you did. Your voice woke me up. You kept saying my name," Inaky explained.

"I swear I didn't call you."

Louis stepped forward to join the conversation. "Hi, I'm Louis, Lilou's father."

"Hello, I'm Inaky, a friend of Lili's."

"Lili?"

"Yes, Inaky calls me Lili."

"Oh, I see! So, Inaky, you heard Lilou calling you?"

"Yes, her voice woke me up. I kept hearing her call my name repeatedly."

"Wow, that's really rare. We've only seen that twice in several decades. We call them 'inseparables,' like birds. Often, they're soulmates. We believe that the same souls come back in each life to reunite and build new generations. You can feel an electric connection between you. It's amazing."

"What's amazing, Louis?" Stella stood behind him.

"Inaky and Lilou are inseparable. Inaky heard Lilou calling him."

"I was just repeating his name in my head. I was thinking about him so he could talk to the birds. Inaky can talk to the birds because his parents and his little brother and sister are owls."

"I have only known two women who have experienced this, Jodelle in the 1600s and Adélaïde in the 1800s. Jodelle and Baldric could not be more than 50 feet apart and felt unwell. Adélaïde and Aimeric felt each other's pain. Every time one was hurt, the other immediately felt the same pain. They could telepathically communicate even when Aimeric died saving his beloved from a bullet destined for her by a Pirate under the influence of Hades. They could communicate through their reflections in the water. Unfortunately, it's a long and beautiful story that you won't be able to learn since your high school might be disrupted and tragically cut short. But we only know of two couples who are true soulmates across time. And we even believe they are the same souls that return once every 200 years."

"So you're saying we would be Jodelle, Baldric, Adélaïde, and Aimeric?"

"I don't know. But for Inaky to hear you calling him when you just said his name in your head, it seems so to me," said Stella.

"Maybe that's why a big flash went through us the first time we saw each other."

"Yes, you're probably right," replied Inaky.

"There was a flash that went through you?"

"Yes, a flash, and I had shivers so big that I felt like the temperature had suddenly changed."

"Come in, Inaky. We need to talk to my mother. By the way, I'm Stella."

"Yes, I know you are our Queen," Inaky crouched down and bowed. "I am truly honored to meet you, My Queen."

"Let's see, you don't have to bow. I'm very pleased to meet my daughter's lover."

"Yes, thank you," he said, embarrassed and red as a tomato.

Lilou took his hand and followed Stella to the living room.

"Wait for me here. I'll fetch my mother."

"Come on, and I need you. We have to talk to our friends. We'll need everyone. I'll explain the plan on the way," Stella said to Louis, pulling him by the arm.

"Don't you find it absolutely wonderful that our daughter is the reincarnation of the greatest ladies ever?"

"Yes, and that she found her other half so quickly. I think it's a sign. This attack will be big, I believe. We absolutely need to prepare well."

Inaky pulled Lili close to him and brushed her lips.

"Did you really hear me call you?"

"Yes, just like I hear you now."

"It's truly wonderful that we're soulmates and were famous lovers before, more than once."

"Yes, it's true. Before I met you, I always felt like there was a void inside me. And the day you set foot on this earth in front of your house, I immediately felt your presence. I came right away to see who you were."

"Was that you in the woods? I also felt your presence immediately, but I had no idea what it was at that moment. Now I understand better."

They kissed tenderly, forgetting they could be caught at any moment by the parents. The flames of the fire increased, and the heat in the room was very intense.

"Wow, you are really souls who are very happy to meet again," said Maminou with a big smile.

Several hours later. After a long discussion, everyone returned to their rooms to prepare for a long day. Inaky also went home to prepare. Isabelle put on comfortable clothes and was ready in an instant. Lilou explained the whole plan to her. They would be trained to replace, not fight, and they would call upon the elders to train them. Unfortunately, a war was looming. She had dreamed of Hades, the King of the Underworld.

"We need to talk to Inaky and the others so they can pass on the message to everyone," Isabelle hurriedly said.

"It's already done. Inaky was with us in the living room."

"When? Right now?"

"Yes, listen carefully to what I have to tell you. He heard me call him, even though I was just saying his name in my head. My mother and Adèle believe we are soulmates who have returned to find each other. We are old souls who have returned twice already because we are inseparable."

"Wow, and that's why you felt the electric shocks."

"I think so, yes."

"That couldn't happen to me." Isabelle was a bit disappointed not to have anything extraordinary.

"I'm sure something really special will happen to you too. Our lives are still young."

"Yes, of course." Isabelle looked sad and disappointed, with a small hint of jealousy towards Lilou. But she quickly forgot about it because she loved her too much.

"So we need to reach out to everyone we know and even those we don't know. We need to warn the animals to prepare for the worst," she said, heading to the back of the courtyard.

"Since when do you talk to animals?" Isabelle asked, following her outside.

"Since forever, I just didn't know it. I thought I was talking like I talk with you and that squirrels spoke our language. Until Inaky overheard me the other day by the water, asking a squirrel to fetch us some hazelnuts. He told me I was speaking their language and that no one else could understand except squirrels."

"Do you speak other animal languages?"

"I speak all animal languages. And..." She hesitated to tell her that she could understand trees. Would she think she's crazy?

"And what?"

"I can understand trees and flowers."

"Like your mother. That must be why the forest is so dense here and the environment is so beautiful. I've never seen so many wildflowers in the forest before."

"Henry told me the other day that his rose bushes hadn't been so beautiful in a long time. Do you really think I have an influence on nature?"

"Not only do I think so, but I'm sure you'll be the greatest queen the earth has ever known."

"What's wrong, Lilou? Bob came to me; he was super stressed, and he told me to come urgently," Inaky said, out of breath from his run.

"Who is Bob?" Isabelle asked Inaky.

"My friend."

"What friend? I don't know any, Bob."

"You asked the squirrel to come talk to me. That I should come back to see you."

"The squirrel is Bob? You named the squirrel your friend, Bob?" Lilou had a giggle on her lips and tried to keep her seriousness. She shouldn't look at Isabelle because she knew she would burst out laughing when she met her gaze.

"Yes, I named my friend the squirrel, Bob. I wanted to give him a little name, and that was the first human name that came to my mind. He's very happy with his human name."

All three of them looked at each other, and an endless laughter echoed through the forest. Lilou had a stomachache. She had to stop laughing and explain the situation. The image of Hades appeared in her head, and the taste for laughter disappeared immediately.

"Yes, when I went to dress, I asked the squirrel to tell you to come back to see me. I absolutely need to talk to you about something important." She narrated her dream in detail, something she hadn't had time to do earlier so that Isabelle would be informed as well. Animals approached. Soon, they were surrounded by all the animals living nearby. Owls, birds of all kinds, and even skunks, otters, and minks were present. Lilou was not distracted by their presence. She finished her story.

"You will be a great Queen, Lilou. Never have I heard that a young initiate could communicate with the underworld so early. We must warn everyone. I will talk to my family."

"When will we start the new teaching procedures?" Isabelle asked with a hint of fear in her voice.

"As soon as the Elders arrive to teach us and everyone has been informed. We would like to have a big meeting in the school gym in two days. I know it doesn't give us much time to gather everyone, but Hades said a few months. If we have two or three months before the attack, we must be ready in a month or two at least."

"We don't have a minute to lose now." Inaky pulled Lilou towards him passionately and kissed her with fervor. Isabelle turned away and walked off to give them some privacy. "I think we won't have much chance to see each other in the coming days. I'll miss you, my beautiful Lili."

"I'll miss you too. Why don't you come see me at nightfall in my room? So we can have a couple of minutes alone."

"Very gladly. My inseparable."

"My parents probably would disapprove, but they don't have to know. We can make sure they don't find out. You'll do your thing and sneak in. Like the other times."

"Do my thing, huh!" They embraced, and Lilou shivered all down her spine.

"I have to go; Isabelle is waiting for me. See you later at school."

"Yes, with the others. Bye." He stepped back a bit, turned around, blew her a flying kiss, and disappeared into the surroundings.

The morning had already passed. Inaky, Lilou, and the whole group were seated in the crowded gymnasium. All the parents answered the call and even brought along neighbors and friends. It was very hard to estimate the number of people present, but there were as many inside as outside. Stella was supposed to speak with a microphone; the men had set up speakers outside so everyone could hear the speech. People were ready to engage in this battle. There were elders present who had already lost loved ones In the last war against Hades and his underworld gang. The day my mother had to leave us. Dad had stayed. He didn't want me to lose both parents if Mom were to die. He had lost both his parents in a war and many friends. We had to end this war and seal the gates of hell forever. Isabelle had lost her parents that day. She must have felt even more involved than I did because I still have mine.

Cats started entering the gymnasium. People wondered what it meant. The gymnasium was soon filled with cats. Ziny, the queen of cats, stopped in front of Stella and meowed several times in a row. Stella looked at her, wondering what to do. She didn't speak cat. She didn't have her translator, Geraldine, with her. She had given her the day off when she returned home, not thinking she would need her.

"There's someone here who speaks cat?" The total silence in the gymnasium was almost scary. Whispers could be heard at the back of the gym. Each person has a cat, but we can understand our own. We can't understand other people's cats. It's really a connection with the cat that chooses you.

"Yes, is there someone? Don't be shy, come." She spotted hair approaching slowly in the crowd. The person was almost there. The cats were following her. Stella recognized her daughter, both hands in the front pockets of her jeans and looking at the floor. "Liliane, do you speak cat?"

"Yes." She had cheeks as red as tomatoes. The pressure suddenly got to her head.

"Wow, never has a future or an apprentice spoken the language of cats before. Except with ours, of course. There's only the mermaid, as we used to call her, who spoke to animals long ago."

"Well, I guess there's a first time for everything."

"Do you speak other languages?"

"I can speak to all animals."

"Well, can you ask what the big tomcat wants?"

"Ziny, her name is Ziny."

"Because he has a name."

"She, Mom, she's a female cat. All cats have a name. We have to give them a name upon arrival when they choose us. Isabelle and I haven't had time to get one yet."

"I named mine Kitty. Can you ask her what she wants, please," said Stella.

Lilou started making noises, and the cat seemed to respond. They meowed like that for a few minutes.

"Ziny says they can also help us in preparing for this war. Cats can perceive the dead. As you know, they can feel the darkness approaching the permitted limit. And you know that Hades hates cats. It could delay him from coming out of his black hole."

"Really interesting. I wouldn't have thought of that. Tell her that any help is welcome. Can they keep us informed of comings and goings or what they might hear from the darkness?"

Lilou translated, "She says they will organize themselves to take turns, and each time there's a change, they will come to warn me or Eva, who also speaks to animals." Lilou pointed at Eva with a smile.

"Perfect, thank you. I would like everyone to split into small groups according to their powers, time powers, emotions, shapeshifters, and those who can control things, like moving objects, changing people's emotions, etc. You will notice on the walls that there are sheets listing powers. Stand in the right place, and an Elder will come to you. You will have long and arduous days in the coming weeks. We are all aware of this, but remember, it's for our collective good. This war must end once and for all. My partner Louis, will take 20 people who want to learn to make weapons. We have the necessary equipment at home. Since the school won't have enough ovens for the premature production of a large number of swords, an Elder will work with half here, and the other half will work with Louis at our home. You may be required to sleep at home or school, so inform your parents where you will be for the next few weeks. One last thing. Those who think this is like a party, staying up late and sneaking out of campus, please leave immediately. Lives will be at stake soon, your parents, close friends, and siblings, we don't have time or energy to waste on you. We have no time to lose. Every second counts. Hades is close to his goal. We are far from ready to face hell. You will be rewarded for your efforts. You will gain freedom and life."

The students were dispersing, and the adults were looking for their children. Panic, fear, and anxiety were starting to be felt in this tiny, crowded gymnasium. Evan closed his eyes and focused on the room's space. Slowly but surely, calm and tranquility settled in. Everyone was whispering, and no one was pushing. He opened his eyes and realized he had succeeded.

"Wow, Evan, your gift is amazing," Isabelle said to him.

"I had never managed to do that before. Until today, I could only change the thoughts or emotions of one person at a time."

"Well, you must practice to prevent people from being afraid on the big day. If they're not afraid, they'll charge ahead, and we'll win."

"Yes, I need to see how far I can project my power, especially the maximum number of people I can control. We can practice together if you'd like."

"Yes, okay, I'd love to. We could start with the distance, see how far you can reach me, and maybe make me laugh. And then, with distance, see how many people you can reach at once."

"It'll be fascinating to work with you," he said, a little embarrassed.

Everyone had their group, as many had more than one gift or a gift that was hard to define. They would change groups daily to practice or improve control of their gift. Lilou didn't know where to go. Stella watched her from afar. She wanted to see what Lilou would decide. She couldn't transform, but she could understand and talk to animals. She could communicate with the earth and nature. She could hear a distant conversation and had a sensational sense of smell. In fact, she didn't know half of her gifts. Lilou was pacing in circles.

"You're going to let her run like this for much longer?" Louis asked Stella quietly.

"I want her to make her own decisions and understand that she has a choice. I don't want her to blame me one day for deciding for her. I'll guide her if she asks me to."

"Okay. Do as you wish. Don't complain if she chooses botany." Louis walked away, glancing back at his daughter. His only daughter, his cherished baby. "Life isn't fair," he thought.

****

Weeks flew by like lightning. Many people had arrived from all over the world to lend assistance and offer their help. Adults and children from other schools, aunts, uncles, and grandparents. Everyone united to end it for good. The lack of sleep was evident on everyone's faces. People were exhausted. Students were afraid; they didn't feel ready to face this monster and its army. The elders had used all their knowledge to prepare them as best they could. A large quantity of potions and ointments had been prepared. The gardens had been stripped of all flowers or spices. There was nothing left. The approaching winter would undoubtedly be the hardest to endure. If they used everything that had been prepared to heal future wounds, reset limbs, stop suffering, etc., it would be very difficult to recover after this war. The absence of herbs, spices, and crops would have been crucial for healing and nourishing the wounded, exhausted, and hungry populace. Rebuilding everything that was ravaged would seem nearly insurmountable. It would undoubtedly require several years to erase this conflict's remnants completely.

Two weeks had already passed. Several swords and armories were ready. The students had truly exceeded their learning capacity. Learning to control and push their powers to the maximum in a few weeks. It was unheard of. The elders had been through many wars and won some victories.

But they knew this one would be different. This group of teenagers had stronger powers; no one before had more than one power at a time. Some could speak to animals, understand nature, and even take its form. For a reason still unknown, everything is different. The gifts are amplified, but not only are they amplified, they are truly greater than ever. Emma and several others can make snow fall even on a beautiful autumn day at 18 degrees Celsius. They tried together to test the strength of their combined power. They made 5 feet of snowfall in the blink of an eye, with strong winds and unbearable cold. Luckily, they quickly snapped their fingers to melt it all with intense heat. We had to mop up water for hours. But at least now we know how strong they are together. They didn't try multiple times. We were too afraid of the consequences. Let's just say they didn't try the wind... A tornado wouldn't have helped matters right now. They helped a lot to make the gardens grow faster, with lots of rain and bright sun. So, we were able to produce more ointments and medicines quickly. Also, to make more food supplies. A group of hungry teenagers eats a lot and often.

Isabelle still doesn't have a power. In any case, she hasn't discovered it yet, if she has one. So, she helps everywhere. In the kitchen, bringing water to everyone. She also learned to make ointments, medicines, herbal teas, and more. Grand-mi taught her a few phrases to calm down people who will be seriously injured. Of course, in Gaelic. It's their language of healing and prayer. It's the language of our ancestors.

"You absolutely must learn these two phrases and memorize them. Repeat them often so you don't forget them. You will need them. 'Èist ris an tsàmhchair agus tuit na chadal. Bheir an latha air ais thu.' "

"What does that mean, Grand-mi?"

"Listen to the silence and fall asleep. The day will bring you back. Repeat this phrase as often as you can so you never forget it. This phrase will soothe the suffering, and the day will bring them back if they don't pass the wall of the dead."

"The wall of the dead?"

"That's what we call it when we die. We cross the wall of the dead, and we can never return. When you think a wounded person won't make it through the night because their injuries are too deep or severe, you must say this phrase."

"Gun co-dhunaidh na ban-diathan d'fhulangas a mhaolachadh no gun tig na h-ainglean agus gun toir iad air ais thu."

"It means, May the Goddesses decide to ease your suffering, or may the angels take you back. You must say this phrase to ensure their safe passage to the wall of the dead if they cannot return from their sleep. We'll repeat them together if you can't say them alone."

"Okay, Grand-mi, count on me, I'll learn them by heart." After a few days, Isabelle recites them by heart. Grand-mi even taught her several other phrases to aid healing. She also taught her a little song that she sang to baby Lilou to lull her to sleep and calm her often disrupted sleep. Even when she was very young, Hades was already speaking to Lilou in her dreams. Grand-mi told her they were just bad dreams and to forget them. That no one would come to harm her or her family.

"That one, Grand-mi, will be harder to learn, but I'll manage."...A brief silence ensued, and Isabelle continued, saying, "By the time I have my own children!" Grand-mi laughed. She understood that Gaelic isn't learned in a day. It's a difficult language that changes words depending on the sentence's meaning. "Would you sing it for me while preparing this ointment that removes scars?"

Cadal mo ghaoil, cadal.

Bidh na h-ainglean a 'cruthachadh an sgiathan os cionn do cheann gu flur.

Chan urrainn don dorchadas sin a dhol thairis.

Cadal mo ghaoil. Cadal.

Eisd ris na h-ainglean a' seinn teagaisgidh iad beatha dhut.

Na seall air an dorchadas chan fhaic thu ach dorchadas.

Cadal mo ghaoil, cadal.

Anns a 'mhadainn bidh thu a' faireachdainn math.

Cadal mo ghaoil, cadal.

"Can you translate it for me, grandma, so I can understand what it says?"

"Of course, this song my mother used to sing it to me to put me to sleep. And I sang it to Stella and Lilou every night to put them to sleep. I even think this song has been around for a really long time."

Sleep my darling, sleep.

The angels will form with their wings a flower above your head.

That the darkness will not be able to cross.

Sleep my darling, sleep.

Listen to the angels singing, they will teach you about life.

Do not look at the darkness, you will only see darkness.

Sleep my darling, sleep.

At the early morning, you will feel good.

Sleep my darling, sleep.

"Wow that's really beautiful. I will sing it one day to my children."

Grand-mi sincerely hoped that rebuilding a new life after this war would be possible. But the chances are so slim. Hades is so powerful that he must have gone to fetch demons from Tartarus, the deepest region of Hell. The hollower they are, the more dangerous they are, too. But the difficulty lies in coming back from there. Hades knows that whenever he descends there, he returns with a thinner layer of life. So closer to true death. Because Hades isn't in hell due to death; he was sent there by his parents, Cronos and Rhea. Since his two brothers before him, Zeus, his elder brother, is the master of the sky. Poseidon, the second, the master of the sea. And his sister, Demeter, the Goddess of nature and earth. At the birth of Hades, only hell remained. He has eternal life, dwelling in the Elysian Fields, the part of hell closest to Earth. But hell is hell. Whoever touches it gets pricked. Hades sent several of his servants, but they could not return. So, if he wanted to have the most powerful ones by his side, Lucifer's servants, he had to go get them himself. So, having been there more than once, because the most powerful ones are also the least obedient. So he had to send back many and obviously take others. The last time he went there, he brought a beautiful little dog with him. A Cerberus. A magnificent big dog with three heads. Nothing less than a dog that doesn't die if you don't cut off the three heads. They are huge, powerful, and often used to pull masters' chariots. They hate cats and make a meal out of them.

This war will surely be the most difficult in every way. Even though we have a large number of brave and quickly trained students. They are still just inexperienced students and teenagers. Which means they often act too quickly without thinking under emotion. There are many of us, but we will probably lose half of us as well. It will be painful to start over.

A month later, since everything was ready, weapons, food, medicine, bandages, and the training of students, to the maximum extent possible in such a short time. Stella called everyone into the gymnasium. People were nervous and agitated. Stella called Lilou with her index finger.

"Tell me, what's the name of your friend who can control emotions?"

"Evan. Why?"

"People are so nervous and anxious that it disturbs me. I feel their fear. I'll ask him if he can calm everyone down."

Stella called Evan to the microphone. He wondered why Lilou's mother, the Queen, was calling him. She whispered in his ear if it was possible for him to calm everyone down.

"Yes, no problem." He complied, and Stella felt an inner calm. The whole room was silent, you could hear everyone's breathing.

"Thank you. Would you mind staying close to me while I speak to everyone?"

"Yes, of course my Queen." He looked at Lilou and her group, shrugging to indicate he didn't quite understand, but he stayed in place, a bit shy.

"Hello, everyone. I am really proud of all of you. We have accomplished something great and even more than great these past few weeks. Never before have I seen students work so hard and learn so quickly with such seriousness and skill. We know what awaits us, but we also know we must defend our land, families, and friends. Know that Hades will show no mercy. Women, children, the elderly, nothing will stop him from destroying everything in his path. Have no pity for Hades, the enemy, no hesitation. The second you spend too much time thinking is the second they will have to kill you. We will be ready in a few weeks. Tonight, we will celebrate. Outside the campfires, we have a piece of beef, a pig, chickens, fruits, nuts, potato salad, drinks, and wine. Eat and celebrate with your loved ones and friends. Tomorrow is another day. Tomorrow brings a new beginning, and we will be victorious. The next few weeks will be crucial. You will need to put into practice what you have learned over the past weeks and learn what you have not yet learned. But most importantly, enjoy your family, friends, and loved ones."

Stella looked at Louis, a tear appearing in the corner of her eye. He climbed onto the stage to join her and hugged her.

"I want to thank all those who prepared this joyful feast and ensured provisions for our survival. Let the celebration begin," Louis said, suggesting Stella take a break as she was struggling to contain her emotions despite Evan's help. Everyone applauded as they headed towards the feast.

"Thank you, Evan, for being here and staying calm. It really helped me a lot," Stella hugged him and thanked him again.

"Don't mention it, my Queen. I'll always be available for you or your daughter Lilou," he said timidly.

The music, laughter, and various discussions livened up the evening. People danced and had fun like never before. Stella moved from group to group, chatting with everyone. She was with her daughter's group. With a heavy heart, she looked at Liliane. So young and full of life. So beautiful.

"Will you introduce me to your friends, Liliane?" She didn't know them all. In recent weeks, she has seen a lot of Inaky and Evan, but not the others, only from afar.

"Of course, Mom. This is Inaky. Do you remember him?"

"Yes, I remember him very well. Are you the one who comes to the house at night?" She said with a smirk.

"Yes, ma'am, I mean, my Queen," Inaky turned beet red.

"Call me Stella. Know that I always know everything. And don't be afraid, I've been young too. What is your power exactly?"

"I can turn invisible. I see in the darkness as if it's daylight, and I can read minds. I also talk to birds."

"Wow, that's amazing. Tell me, what is Isabelle thinking right now?" Inaky tried to read her mind.

"How do you do that?"

"I do what?" Isabelle asked.

"I'm not reading anything at all. It's like trying to read the thoughts of a dead person."

"What? I have the thought of a dead."

"But no, I'm absolutely not capable of reading your thoughts. It's like a black hole."

"Evans, try to make her cry," said Stella.

"Nothing. I can't get inside her. I can neither make her cry nor make her laugh. This has never happened to me before."

"Wow, I've never seen that before. It must be your human half that's making it not work," Stella tried to explain, not quite understanding herself. "You come from grandparents who are half human and half wizard, maybe that's it," Stella thought.

"Yes, that must be it, at least to you. We can never do anything to you," he said, pointing at Inaky. "You can think whatever you want, no one will ever know. No one will be able to control you either, lucky," said Evan, trying to make her understand that he wasn't controlling his emotions. He was trying to lighten the mood and see the bright side. He could see that Isabelle was wondering.

"I think you're a protector. Like a kind of shield," replied Lilou.

"A protector. Maybe that's why I always feel the immense need to protect you and stay by your side. And as you say, a kind of shield, so that's why Inaky can't read my thoughts, and Evan can't control my emotions," she said, realizing he couldn't control his emotions. So what she felt for him were true feelings and not Evan's control, making her madly in love. She grabbed him by the neck and planted a kiss on his mouth. "I'm crazy about you, but I thought you were trying to control my emotions." Evan, taken by surprise, said nothing at all.

"Evan, say something." Inaky nudged him with an elbow. Evan looked at him and gave a huge smile.

"Finally, she understood I was just waiting for this moment."

"Love It's so beautiful," said Stella. "So, you are the protector of my daughter. Your parents were my protectors. I really loved them a lot. They were great warriors. They saved us. It is thanks to them that we are all here today. They were my best friends too."

"Yes, I know. They told me in my dream the night of my initiation."

"It's good that you could see and talk to them. So, who are the other people with you, Liliane?"

"You know Eva. She speaks and understands all animals through thought. She can also change into the animal of her choice."

"Really interesting. Nice to meet you, Eva."

"Mathieu, he moves objects. He recently learned that he could even move a fairly large rock and replant a tree without damaging it. He is Emma's lover. Emma controls the weather. She can whip up a tornado with a snap of her fingers or even make 5 feet of snowfall in a blink of an eye."

"I didn't make 5 feet of snowfall all by myself; we were 4," she said shyly.

"I'm sure you could do it if you had to," Stella said, having observed her earlier in the week. "Nice to meet you, lovers."

"It's really an honor to meet you, Stella. My mother used to put me to sleep with stories about you every night when I was little," Emma timidly said.

"Me too," said Mathieu, taking Emma by the waist. "I believe our generation has had the right to hear your stories every night because our parents are grateful to be here with us, thanks to you."

"I wasn't alone, you know. You were also saved by extremely courageous people who gave their lives to save yours, like Isabelle's parents. They didn't hesitate for a second to throw themselves into Hades' arms to prevent him from crossing to our side. Louis's parents,

Liliane's father, and many other relatives, children, and grandparents were also there. We have lost many people in recent wars, and we will surely lose as many in this one. But this time, we will close the gates of hell forever."

"What makes you say that? Why do you believe we will succeed this time?" Mathieu asked, curious.

"Because you are all different from what we have known so far. You are ten times more powerful than we were as adults, trained for several years. The children looked at each other proudly, knowing they were the generation that would stop Hades once and for all. My daughter has the soul of the two strongest women we have ever known and will be the most powerful ever seen. She is already ready to replace me if I were to die. She has Inaky, her sweet half, and Isabelle, her protector. And she has all of you. You will be in good hands."

"Mom, you're not going to die, don't say that, please. No one will die. We will be victorious."

"We hope so, my dear."

"And there's also Marc. Inaky's cousin is an owl man. It's handy for night surveillance. Inaky's family they're practically all owls. That's why they have yellow eyes and can see very well in the night. Inaky inherited their eyes."

"That's really handy. We'll definitely need you. So, Marc and Eva are together? Since they're the only ones left?"

"Yes, they are together."

"It makes a solid team. I wish you all good luck, enjoy this evening and have fun. Inaky, you can come to sleep over tonight, but please use the front door this time and not my daughter's window like a thief," she said with a wink.

Inaky was as red as a strawberry and stammered to reply. "I... I... yes, of course. Thank you, Stella. I won't use the window again, I promise."

"Perfect, good evening to all of you," she gracefully walked away in her long, sun-yellow veiled dress and joined her husband. She paused for a moment and turned back. "Inaky, would you please come with me for a moment?"

"Yes, of course, no problem." He kissed Lili and joined Stella. "Walk with me for a moment, will you?"

"Yes, okay." His legs suddenly felt weak. *What could she possibly want to tell me?* He turned and glanced at Lilou. She was looking at him with concern and questions in her eyes.

"I'm really happy that Liliane found you. Or that you found each other."

"Yes, me too. I'm happy to have found her."

"Does she really know who you are?"

"No, I don't think she really understands who we are. But how do you know?"

"I felt it in your presence the first time I saw you at the entrance of our house. I felt all your past, your ancient sufferings, and the power of your love. I had heard about you, we studied your lives in our school courses. But I didn't believe it was true or possible. Goddess, my daughter, is the reincarnation of divinity. She will be the greatest Queen who has ever existed. She has such great power and doesn't even know half of it. I will have to teach her what she needs to know about herself in the coming days...

How can I gently introduce the incredible abilities she possesses? She can communicate with animals and hold sway over them, commanding their obedience even in the ocean's depths. She wields the power to rejuvenate a lifeless tree wherever she chooses. She can influence the life cycles of all living beings, even time itself. The challenge lies in conveying these extraordinary truths without causing her undue alarm."

"By telling her the truth as it is. I must explain to her who we really are, me too. It won't be easy. It's the same every time. I remember everything, but I don't know why she always returns without memories. I have to transmit them to her again each time. And every time, it's painful."

"You are her other half, so you will have to protect her, as always."

"Yes, but this time, I'm not leaving without her. The solo passage through the wall of death is over."

"You can't do that."

"It's out of the question for me to leave this earth again without her, only to return before her and endlessly search for her."

"You must protect and sacrifice yourself for her at all costs."

"Not this time. I'll stay on earth with her, or she'll come back with me."

"Then make sure to stay because we'll need her here."

"I'll talk to her tonight. Tomorrow, she'll know who she truly is."

"All right. Thank you, Inaky, for taking care of my daughter."

"That's normal. That's what I'm here for. She's my whole life. Or rather, all my lives."

"How is it possible to love someone, life after life, and love them so much?"

"It's a feeling that can't be explained. It's like a tree needing water to survive. I couldn't survive without her. She's essential for my survival, just as I am for hers."

"Wow, it's still incredible that you find each other every time. Do you have the same age in each life?"

"Approximately, yes. Each time, I was in a different place, in a different era, with different parents and constraints. And even though we only come back once every 200 years, it feels like we were separated just yesterday. Time is completely different on the other side of the death wall. Well, there's not really time. We don't age anymore, and there's no illness either. It's like it's always the same day but moving forward at the same time. It's really hard to explain like this. What I'm trying to say is that for me, I left her yesterday to find her again today in another place in another era. But we always have the same appearance, just in different styles of clothing."

"You mean you always have the same appearance."

"Yes, of course, it's easier to recognize each other that way. Even though this time, she really doesn't recognize me. I don't know why."

"Wow, that's incredible. You should tell your story."

"I think people know it," replied Inaky with a slight smile.

"No, we learned about it from books. We've never had the chance to meet you and hear the real version. There are so many details we don't know, like how your appearance stays the same and the fact that you always come back first. We don't know the real story. When all this is over, you have to tell us your story to help us better understand where we come from and why you exist."

"Okay, let me help her regain her memory and accept what's happening. And then I'll talk to her. I'll explain who we really are tonight. And I'll be happy to share our story after this war."

"Okay, no problem."

Inaky was about to leave when Stella grabbed his arm.

"Thank you, Inaky."

"Of what?"

"To take care of my daughter, I haven't seen her grow up until today. I would really like to see her grow old."

"I will do everything in my power to protect her again and again, I promise you. And many of us are here to protect her. Everything will be fine."

Stella went to join Louis, sitting by the fire with a plate in one hand and a glass of wine in the other.

"They are all really beautiful, aren't they?" Louis said, hugging her. "I can't imagine that we could lose them or die and not see them grow old."

"We mustn't think about it because it takes my breath away. Already, I haven't seen her become the extraordinary woman she is. I wouldn't want also not to see her become the future Queen and have her own family." Stella had tears in her eyes and held her husband close. This war was going to be devastating for everyone. Their lives were going to be overturned entirely. She emptied her husband's glass of wine in one gulp.

"Wow, your mom allowed your boyfriend to sleep over at your place. My mom would never accept such a thing," Eva said.

"Did you ask her?"

"No, I know her very well. She would never accept such a thing."

"Can I come too then?" Evan asked. Since Isabelle lived with her, he thought he could sleep with his beloved.

"Yes, of course, but it's just for sleeping. Only sleeping. Do you understand the message, right?" Isabelle replied.

"Yes, don't worry, I'll be a true gentleman. I just want to spend as much time as possible with you since we might die soon."

 "Hey, we're not going to die, you know. We're strong, fast, and well-prepared," Isabelle replied eagerly.

"We shouldn't think about that," Lilou said.

"But most importantly, we're smarter and more patient. We don't want to conquer at any cost. We want to live. I think that's what makes the difference between Hades and us," said Marc, he had immense confidence in himself and his friends. He's the positive one in the group. The one who always says yes and encourages everyone.

Inaky joined them again.

"I wonder what your mother had to say to him," Isabelle whispered in Lilou's ear.

"Me too. And I don't know her well enough to have any idea what it could be," Lilou replied.

Inaky approached and kissed his sweetheart.

"What did she say?" Lilou asked, concerned.

"I'll tell you later. Let's enjoy the party for now. It's in our honor, so we all should make the most of it," Inaky suggested.

"Okay, but at least tell me if it was positive or negative?"

"Positive. And your mother is very kind. She loves you a lot, contrary to what you think." Inaky reassured her.

"I know. Let's go dance."

"I don't know how to dance this dance."

"Then you must learn."

The evening ended very late. No one wanted this day to end because nothing would ever be the same again from the next day onward.

The bagpipe, the banjo, the accordion, the violins, and the cello created a lovely, lively music. The mulled wine, the meat cooked over the fire, and the fruits made a complete and delicious meal. Everyone was dancing, laughing, and eating with gusto. The past few weeks had been so long and exhausting that all of this was more than appreciated. People were eating more than they could, afraid of not having time to eat in the coming weeks. Several people had fallen asleep in the gym on the exercise mats. Too exhausted. Some had already gone home, and others were taking their families back before returning to sleep. The older ones were putting out the campfires for safety. They were less tired and still able to stand, putting away the leftovers. Nothing should be wasted.

The next few weeks will be tough, but not as tough as the ones we just went through. The first week was truly exhausting. We only slept a few hours a night because of the training. We were so stressed and anxious that we wanted to work day and night and not waste a single moment of our preparation. Some collapsed and lost consciousness. Others cried for fear of losing their family and friends. With stress and fatigue, it's completely normal.

My father sometimes lacked patience and immediately apologized. He then took the time to sit down to remember why they were all there. The students encouraged him by saying they forgave him, as they, too, were upset and exhausted. So Louis would stand up again and continue teaching about weapons. Swords, bows, daggers, and shields were taught to them in such a short time. My father had spent a lifetime learning it all and forging a perfect sword. While they only had a few weeks. When he returned to his room in the evenings, he started putting everything on paper. Everything he had learned from his father and everything Alfred had taught him after his death.

That way, if he were to die, the children would have a book to refer to. The mandatory lengths, the ideal weight for each weapon, preferred materials, and where to get them. Cooking methods and practical advice.

Several burned themselves while making the weapons. Melting and recovering the metal with the forge wasn't as easy as it seemed, some more than others. The stronger ones had less difficulty than the skinny ones. But no less determination. The ointment makers were put to the test. They quickly saw if their ointment worked or not. Some were more skilled than others, but that's true in all groups. A few of them were truly gifted, while others had to work even harder, but in the end, everyone achieved the same result. One of the apprentice armorers cut a finger, and Isabelle was able to reattach it. She learned very quickly and discovered a passion for potions. Some swords were forged a bit too heavy. Actually, it's way too heavy. One was so heavy that it took two people to lift it. Louis had to melt it down to make two new ones. This story will be told, told, and told again over the years. At least there will be funny memories from this war, like in the potions, ointments, and natural remedies class. One of the girls made a tea blend for relaxation and made her best friend try it. She had diarrhea for two days straight. She hadn't mixed the right ingredients. She had read 'relaxing' on the label, but it actually said 'loosening.' Thank goodness her friend forgave her, but she still had a little revenge in her heart, just for laughs.

My gang and I are sitting on the ground around a fire and don't feel like parting. I'm so snug against Inaky, belly full and warm near the crackling fire. Stella is walking toward us. She's so beautiful in her long-sun dress, her long hair, and magnificent eyes. My parents looked really good together. My father is a very handsome man, tall and strong, with pale chestnut hair and light blue eyes. Many women have tried to catch his attention in recent years. Widows, divorced, and even married ones make him a great lover. Yuck! Even my old school principal from before often asked if my father had found someone. I always said yes. Can you imagine the school principal as a stepmother? NOOOO!! That couldn't happen.

I imagined myself going to school accompanied by my stepmother... And everyone was looking at me and not daring to speak to me. No, impossible! There was no question of Mrs. Clara becoming my stepmother. There was also the lady from the post office whom my father saw every week when he went to pick up his orders, the lady from the deli, and many others. My father could have had many women if he had wanted someone by his side. But he was waiting for my mother. He knew she would come back. It's not fair, all this time when I thought she was dead. I understand why now, anyway, I'm trying to understand. But I would still have liked my father to trust me enough to tell me this secret.

"Good night, children," Stella said softly. "Don't come back too late; you can all come and sleep at our house. I've talked to your parents, and we agree that it's better for Liliane's safety. May you never be apart from now on. There are several guest rooms available. And several sofas, too."

"Mama, nobody calls me Liliane; everyone calls me Lilou."

"Except me!" Inaky replied.

"Yes, but you're different," I said, kissing him.

"I love the name I chose for you. Liliane was your great-grandmother's second name, and she was a great lady."

"Okay, okay, I get it. Thanks for my friends, but do I really need this much protection?"

"No, not really. But I thought it was the most truthful and safest excuse to get the parents to agree to let them all sleep at the house for the next few weeks."

"Did you lie, Mom?"

"Yes, but it's not a big lie. It's still true that you need to stay together to prepare well and protect yourself. But maybe not to this extent. A little naughty lie never hurt anyone!" she said with a wink.

"Thank you, Mrs Stella," said Eva.

"Just Stella, please, no Mrs. And it brings me extreme pleasure. Enjoy every little moment of laughter and happiness. Tomorrow is another day. We'll need to speed up the learning process and be truly ready to face the darkness."

"We'll be ready, Stella, no worries," said Marc, hugging Eva.

"Perfect, then have a good evening and come finish the night at our place instead; there are hardly any people left here except for a few very beat-up ones. Make a fire outside, but come to the house. I'll be more reassured."

"Yes, okay, we'll come, Mom. We'll be right behind you two."

Everyone got up and gathered their belongings, then walked to Lilou's house. Luckily, it's only a little over a kilometer's walk. It's a nice walk that will help keep them awake. It was dark, and the moon was almost completely hidden, not lighting the path much.

"It's rare for the moon to be this hidden. We can hardly see where we're walking," Isabelle said, holding Evan close.

"Yes, not all of us have Inaky and Marc's eyes. You should walk in front of us so we know where to go," Evan said, letting them pass in front of him while making owl noises. "HOO, HOO, HOO!"

"It's true that we don't distinguish between day and night. Let the best ones pass, please," Inaky said, playfully pushing Evan to tease him. The boys started play-fighting in the middle of the street. Evan jumped on Inaky's back, and Marc grabbed Evan's legs. They all ended up sitting on their backsides, tangled together and laughing like crazy.

"They're just kids, these poor guys," Isabelle said, wrapping her arms around the girls.

"Yes, and tomorrow, they will have to become men. It won't be an easy task..." The girls burst out laughing.

A noise rang out in the depths of the night, a distant, muffled sound.

"Goodness, what is that?" Eva went to join Marc and asked the boys to listen for a moment. They hadn't heard anything in their fights. The noise persisted.

"What is that?"

"I don't know, it sounds like children crying," Evan said, closing his eyes to concentrate better. "No, they're not children." They all listened carefully.

"It's the cats meowing," Inaky recognized the sound cats make when there's a problem. "The cats are warning us of danger." Inaky took Lilou's hand and turned to his friends. "Let's hold hands so we don't stray from each other since it's pitch black, and run to the house, please."

"Inaky, I'm scared, what's happening?" Lilou was trembling all over.

"The cats must have spotted someone approaching from the darkness, and they're warning us to hide."

"Eva, can you hear what they're saying?" Isabelle asked.

"No, they're too far away." She glanced at Lilou. Lilou understood that she was asking if she could hear.

"Friends, I have to tell you a secret that only Isabelle, Eva, and I know, as well as my mother. We discovered it a few weeks ago. I didn't want to talk to anyone about it because I didn't know how to handle it. So, I preferred not to talk to anyone immediately. But now I think it's time to tell you."

"Come on, tell us, what is it?" Isabelle was getting impatient.

"I can talk to animals, and they understand me like Eva." She was waiting for her friend's reaction, and they all sighed in relief.

"I was scared; I thought you were going to tell us some very bad news. I'm not surprised at all since you're the future Queen," Evan said, relieved.

"But I speak the language of animals. Eva speaks to them telepathically, and I speak their language. I feel like I speak the same language every day when I talk to them. But when you hear me talking to them, you hear some incomprehensible language."

"Wow, so you can talk to skunks? Bees? Mosquitoes?" Emma said, looking amazed.

"Yes, I don't understand how I do it. I feel like I'm speaking just like now, but you hear a jumble of sounds."

"That's really cool and practical to have two people who can talk to bears in case we get attacked," Evan said, laughing.

"There are no bears around here, you idiot," Isabelle said, nudging him.

"Yes, but you never know," he replied.

"So, can you understand what they're saying?" Inaky asked calmly, taking her hands.

"I'll try." She closed her eyes and focused on the meows. She could hear the meows very clearly. But she didn't know how to understand their meaning. She jumped and startled everyone.

"Oh my goodness, Lilou, what's happening?" Isabelle asked, approaching her. "You scared me."

Lilou stared into Isabelle's eyes, a cold sweat on her neck.

"Did you hear that voice? Lilou was scared."

"What voice? We only hear meows."

"The voice calling my name? You don't hear it?"

"No. Lilou, focus and listen to what this voice wants to tell you," Inaky said.

"Eva, help me." They held hands, and Eva heard the words more clearly.

"The girls opened their eyes in incredible synchrony, stared at each other, and understood that their powers were stronger together."

"The cats say that Hades has come closer. He now knows about Lilou's presence and strength. That among us is a traitor here to spy on behalf of Hades. That Hades knows Lilou is a hundred times stronger than her mother and that she has an army with her." Eva and Lilou wrinkled their brows in confusion at this message.

"An arm..."

"*Shh!!!*" Inaky gestured to Marc, placing a finger over his lips.

"Hades has descended to train more warriors, fearing he may not have enough to fight us. They say we must prepare because Hades will do everything to destroy the future Queen before she can take her throne. They say this gives us a few more weeks before the attack. Hades has, has a Cerberus?!? The cats say Hades has a Cerberus."

"Oh my Goddess, protect us!" Inaky lost his balance, and Evan turned white as snow.

"What's a Cerberus?" Isabelle, Evan, and Emma asked simultaneously.

"A Cerberus is a hellhound. It guards the Styx, the entrance to hell. It only feeds on fresh human meat. And as far as I know, it's the biggest beast that exists. It's larger than an elephant and incredibly cruel."

"And you forgot to mention it has three heads," Marc added.

"What else did the cats say?"

"They heard the message, but no one revealed it. It was a 'bullage.' What's a bullage?"

"It's a magical message. It's like a bubble, only the recipient can pierce it to hear the bubble and message: bullage. You have to be very skilled in magic to do that. I don't know anyone who can do this kind of enchantment," explained Inaky.

"We're all going to die. We're all going to die," Isabelle cried, so panicked that Evan had to calm her down.

"Calm down, Isabelle. We're not going to die. Not today, at least," Evan tried to reassure her, unable to calm her with his powers.

"We must warn my parents at all costs." They heard running footsteps, and panic gripped them. It was so dark. They screamed in panic and all ran together. They saw Lilou's parents.

"Why are you shouting like that, kids?" Louis panicked, thinking something had happened.

"We heard your running footsteps and got scared."

"We were starting to get really worried. You told us you'd be right behind us, and you weren't coming. I was crazy worried," Stella struggled to breathe as she had been so scared hearing them shout like that. Evan calmed her, knowing that what she would hear in a moment would really make her panic.

Lilou glanced at Inaky and turned to face her parents.

"We stopped to listen to the cats' call."

"The cats' call? What cats' call?"

"You didn't hear the cats' call? Lilou and Eva were skeptical. How could you not hear the call, Mom? You're the Queen?"

"I didn't hear anything," Stella paused for a moment. "It's true, and I don't feel anything. Nothing at all. I don't feel the earth under my feet anymore or the vibrations of nature."

"The wine," Louis looked at his wife. "You drank my wine at the end of the evening, remember? You never drink usually."

"Yes, that's true. What was in your wine?"

"I don't know. I didn't drink it, but you finished my glass."

"You've been poisoned. Dad, where did you get this wine?"

"A man brought it to me. He said, 'Here you go, sir, a good glass of homemade wine to celebrate our upcoming victory.'"

"Who was this man, Dad?" Lilou panicked, her whole body trembling.

"I don't know, I didn't really look at him. I was watching people dance, so I just took the glass and said thank you."

"Marc, can you look into his thoughts? Is it possible for you to see the man's face if you look into his thoughts?"

"I don't know, I've never done that, but I can try. We have nothing to lose by trying!" Marc took Louis's hands and closed his eyes.

"Think of the man and try to see him again. Replay the moment when he gave you the glass and your eyes met."

Louis concentrated and replayed the moment when he was watching people dance, and they heard the man's voice: "Here, a good glass of red wine to celebrate our victory, sir." At that moment, Marc recognized the voice and saw the man's face. He opened his eyes and looked at Stella.

"I've never done that before. I was able to read the man's thoughts when your eyes met. He put poison in the wine; he wanted to eliminate you to weaken Lilou with grief."

"Stella, you're poisoned. We need to go see your mother right away."

"Yes, but the poisons on me only slow down or cancel out my powers, luckily. But if you had drunk it, you would be dead. My love, you would be dead. Someone tried to eliminate you to slow us down."

"Mr. Louis, what did he look like?"

"Small, skinny, not very old. But not young, either. Extremely aged hands. He had a smell, I don't know. Smelled like a stable. And I didn't see him again; he just disappeared."

"I recognized him. Marc was looking down. He was as white as snow. He's our chemistry teacher. Lord, a teacher."

"That's why he's so good with potions," Louis replied.

"But Lilou, tell me what the message said. What did the cats say?"

"Let's go home, please. I'm afraid to stay here, and I'll tell you everything once we're home."

The whole group huddled together and approached Lilou's parents. Evans kept calm all around, but they all knew their bodies were truly in panic, even if they didn't feel it. Gradually, Stella regained her senses. When they arrived home, she made tea. But of course, not knowing which poison was more difficult. She looked at her husband, whom she could have lost a few hours earlier. He looked up at that moment and saw the fear in his wife's eyes. He pushed the chairs to go to her on the other side of the table and took her in his arms. He hugged her so tightly that Stella had difficulty breathing. She didn't mind at all because she thought she would rather die from her husband's caress than anything else.

"Lilou, I need to talk to you privately."

"I have to tell my parents what happened first. You can talk to me later."

"Okay, but it's very important."

"Okay, go ahead, I'm listening."

"No, it won't take 2 minutes."

"How so?"

"Because what I must tell you will take longer than two minutes. I need to talk to you about us. To explain certain things. To explain where we come from and why there's electricity between us when we're really close."

"Okay. I'll explain everything to my parents, and we'll go talk in my room."

Louis started a fire, and Stella went to prepare glasses of warm milk with honey for everyone to relax a little. Lilou recounted in detail everything she had heard with Eva to her mother and father. Her grandparents came to join them, and after Stella explained about the poison in the wine, Adèle prepared a wildflower tea with Lapacho bark. Stella regained all her senses after several minutes. The earth vibrated beneath her feet again, and the pulsations of nature vibrated throughout her entire body.

"Finally, everything returned to normal. I was scared for a moment."

"It really wouldn't be the time for you to lose your powers. We would lose this war quickly," Lilou said, relieved.

"No, my dear. We wouldn't lose since you're here."

"I'm not like you, Stella. I don't have your powers. It's not by talking to the cat or being able to hear them that I could push Hades away."

"No, that's true. That wouldn't help you. But you have all your friends who are very strong by your side. And you have great powers, you're just not aware of them yet." Lilou stood up suddenly and shouted at the top of her lungs.

"And do you think not being aware of having great power, as everyone seems to believe, will make me the one who pushes back Hades for good? Do you think I'll wake up one morning and be a nature superwoman with incredible powers? You're dreaming, and you're expecting an impossible thing from me. Stop thinking I'm the solution. Because I don't believe it."

Lilou ran out of the room, took the stairs two at a time, slammed her bedroom door behind her, and fell onto her bed. She was so angry, sad, and scared. Inaky came a few minutes later to talk to her.

Lilou was sitting on her bed with her head in her hands and her knees folded on her stomach. She didn't quite understand what Inaky had just told her. The surprise, the story, was that she didn't really know what to call it all. She went over the key phrases in her head and tried to put them together to make sense. She couldn't imagine that she was someone who had lived several lives before this one and moreover with Inaky each time. Lilou looked at him; his face was the new face that she had discovered a few months earlier in the forest. She had never seen him before. She would have recognized him. For example, when you see someone at the mall, you have a logical reaction by raising your arm to greet them. Or by taking them in your arms and asking them, "Hey, how are you?" No, his face was not familiar to her at all. She had never seen it before. She was absolutely, absolutely sure of it.

"It's not possible, and I don't know you, Inaky. I've only known you for a few months, not centuries. What you're telling me really doesn't make any sense."

"I swear it's true. Normally you should have regained all your memory by drinking the sacred water at your initiation. I don't know why it didn't work this time. It's the same for me, you know. I come into the world in the same body every time. In a family, I don't know. I find memory in each life at my initiation, and I must find you first each time because I always come into the world before you."

"What you're saying is completely crazy."

"I know. But it's the truth."

"Am I still in love with you? In every life, I fall in love with the same person. I always relive the same life," she exclaimed. "There's never any change; everything is always the same every time. Are my parents still the same parents?"

"It depends on how you see it. But yes, your mother is still the same. Her soul is like yours, always coming back but not necessarily in the same body as your grandmother or great-grandmother. You are the supreme queens, and each life brings you more knowledge and strength. That's why Stella is convinced that we can defeat Hades this time. Because your last life brought you knowledge about Hades and how he operates. Just like Stella. You can defeat him this time."

"But I don't remember anything. I can only talk to animals and hear them talk."

"You haven't regained your powers yet, but they are deep within you." Inaky placed his index finger on Lilou's chest, looking into her eyes. "You just need to know how to retrieve them."

"Just need to know how to retrieve them. Do you think it's like a guessing game or something? That I just have to talk to myself and say, 'Powers, appear...'"

"No, of course not. But they are somewhere within you. Let's go see your mother and grandparents, maybe they know how or what to do."

"Yes, that's it. My grandmother will make me tea, and then I'll be able to conjure up a fire or move a tree."

"I love your humor, Lilou."

"Even better, that way, if I don't have powers, I can always try to get into humor," I replied sarcastically.

They went down to the living room, hoping to find answers. Upon arriving, Lilou stopped at the bottom of the door.

"What's wrong, Lilou?" Inaky, behind her, glanced into the room.

Nobody. There was no one left. Everyone had gone to bed a while ago. But no one had dared to go and tell them and disturb them in their big discussion.

"They went to sleep, and we should do the same, we'll be really tired tomorrow at school."

"Tomorrow is Saturday, Lilou. You can sleep in."

"That's great, then. Come on, let's go to sleep."

...a brief silence, and a big question mark formed on Inaky's face.

"Yes, I did say come on, WE are going to sleep. Remember, you're sleeping here with me. My nice mom allowed everyone to sleep here."

"Yes, yes, I remember. I just forgot with everything going on. Don't worry, I won't keep you awake. I'd be too afraid you'd turn me into an ant."

"Could I turn you into an ant?" Lilou struggled to swallow as she asked the question.

"I don't know. Each time, your powers are different and stronger."

"Idiot. You scared me. It's too much. It's too much for me. And if I had that power, I think I'd do worse to you than turning you into an ant."

"What could be worse than being turned into an ant?"

"A mouse!"

...??? He wondered.

"Your family are owls, right? So, they eat mouse from time to time. How will they know it's you and not eat you?"

"You wouldn't do that?"

"It could be fun to see you running and shouting, 'don't eat me, don't eat me, it's me, Inaky!!' And with all of the cats around... I hope you run fast."

"No, that wouldn't be funny at all. You wouldn't do that to me for real, right?"

"No, of course not. I'm not that mean. But it would still be funny, I think," I said as I climbed the stairs.

Lilou's night was troubled and restless. Inaky held her in his arms to reassure her and help her calm down. The sun was shining high in the sky when Lilou opened her eyes. Barely out of sleep, she realized Inaky was sleeping next to her. She had forgotten that slightly embarrassing detail. She turned gently to face him. Propping herself up on her elbow, she observed him for a moment. How beautiful he is. His perfect skin. His perfect nose and lips, hmm, lips as enticing as raspberry pink hearts. His ebony hair is soft as silk. His slightly tanned skin was without any imperfections. He's so handsome. Lilou began to think. She's been in love with this boy for many lifetimes. It's unbelievable, these things can't happen for real. Like if we could really come back into another body while remaining ourselves and fall in love with the same person each time but with a different body. A different appearance and in different places. I must have dreamed, it doesn't make sense. She watched him in silence and kissed his raspberry-pink lips. Inaky opened his eyes, and their gazes met.

Lilou had a flash. She saw herself hand in hand with Inaky in a lavender field. A round wooden house. A white house filled with children around a large table. Inaky seated across from her. He looks the same each time but with slight differences. Longer or shorter hair, depending on the time, probably. She felt the fears or joys of those years. Inaky watched her, wondering what she was seeing. He knew she was reliving the past years and realizing her powers. Finally, he thought.

"Inaky, did we have children?" Lilou's eyes were full of tears. I don't remember anything except that I saw us hand in hand in a lavender field with a white wooden house. That's all I had a flash of, but I don't remember you or many of our lives, just that moment."

"Yes, in each of our lives, we've had children. And we were happy."

"But, what if I had fallen in love with Evan, let's say? What would you have done?"

"I would have waited for you."

"Just like that?"

"Yes, just like that. But you couldn't have fallen in love with Evan."

"Why is that?"

"Because you're crazy about me, my love. And I wouldn't have let you."

"Do you really think I can't fall in love with someone other than you?"

"Yes, I'm certain."

"You're way too sure of yourself. You know what? That would be a challenge I'd like to take on. But it can't be Evan. So I'll have to find a super handsome young man and fall in love to prove you wrong."

"I'd love to see that. Watching you try to love someone other than me will be hilarious. No matter how hard you try, it'll be impossible for you not to think of me."

"Hmm, you're really too sure of yourself. Come on, let's go eat. I need to find this great guy. I should call Nathan to see if he's free and if he'll be around our area soon!"

"Who is Nathan?"

"Such a handsome young man who used to go to my old school. He was my first kiss in this life." I walked down the steps quickly, so there was no time to ask me any other questions about Nathan. I wanted him to have doubts.

The house smelled of strawberry muffins and good coffee. The table was filled with muffins, a huge fruit salad, freshly baked croissants, freshly squeezed orange juice, and a coffee carafe. Everyone at the table was talking with their mouths full. Mr. Henry's breakfasts are always so excellent that we can't help but talk while eating so we are not missing a single bite. Suddenly, the silence was heavy in the room. Everyone was looking at Inaky.

"...," the eyes shifted from Inaky to Lilou. Her father raised his eyebrows, a big question mark appearing on his face.

"He slept with me, it was very late. And we slept. Mom allowed him to sleep here like everyone else, remember?"

"Don't worry, Mr. Louis, I was just sleeping. We only slept, I promise!"

"A very wise decision," Louis replied, winking at Inaky. The conversation resumed vigorously. No other comments were made. Only one subject surrounded the table that morning. Various ideas, disagreements, and questions revolve around the same topic. Hades!! Everyone greatly appreciated the weekend. They were exhausted, no training, no classes this weekend, just a rest. Everyone deserved it. The young people sat around the fire outside with big, warm blankets, some even stayed to sleep outside in sleeping bags. Lilou was trying to light the fire, but nothing seemed to work. Her thoughts, finger movements, and words like 'Fire, light up. Light yourself fire.' Nothing worked. She was discouraged.

"I have no talent. I can't do anything."

"Do you remember when you hit me with a branch this summer?"

"Sure, I remember that."

"So, how did you do it?"

"I closed my eyes and asked the tree to push you gently."

"There you go. Close your eyes and ask the fire to light up."

Lilou looked at him skeptically. She closed her eyes and asked the fire to light up. Lilou followed Inaky's idea. WIth her eyes closed, she said in her mind: "Fire, light up to warm us." A huge flame illuminated and rose at least six feet in the air. Everyone jumped in their seats, stood up, and moved away from the blazing fire.

"Wow, Lilou, you'll set the forest on fire if you keep going."

She felt the warmth of the fire even before opening her eyes, she knew she had succeeded.

"See, I knew you had great powers. The branch this summer not only touched me, but it propelled me. You just had to ask for it to work. Clearly, your powers are and will be the greatest ever seen." Said Inaky with admiration.

"You have to trust yourself. Your powers are within you, you have to let them surface," Emma said.

"But I don't know how."

"Like you did with the branch and the fire. You stay calm and ask them for help. You have to tell them that you need them, and they have to help you," Isabelle said with great confidence in her friend.

"Try it. Try to extinguish the fire and then relight it," Marc suggested.

"Okay." With her eyes closed, Lilou ordered the fire to extinguish itself. Suddenly, the heat disappeared. No more flames. "Relight." The warmth reappeared instantly.

"See, you're capable of everything. You'll be exceptional." Inaky, his eyes shining with admiration, stretched to kiss her. "Correction, you are exceptional. You have your gifts within you, they're just shy."

They stayed there sleeping all night. Since Lilou could now keep the flame lit, no one would be cold. The night was cool, but they were very comfortable with the fire and wrapped in blankets. The starry sky and the moon were very clear. Lilou's sleep was undisturbed. She dreamed of her past lives and saw Inaky in several forms, but always resembling each other. It's sweet how Inaky encourages Lilou and how they enjoy the night together.

****

Lilou was very quiet at breakfast on Monday morning. No one dared to ask if everything was okay. Just before leaving the room to go to school, where they all had to resume training, Lilou turned around to face everyone and took a deep breath.

"I need to express myself this morning. I want to talk to everyone. I have things to say. I feel inside me that I need to speak to everyone. When we arrive at school, I want to convey the message through the cats so that everyone receives the message. I felt a great need to express myself when I woke up this morning. It's like I dreamed of a speech, and now I must deliver it."

"You talked all night, Lili, I'm not surprised," said Inaky.

"Really?"

"Yes, I absolutely understood nothing of what you were saying. It was as if you were speaking another language."

"*Labhair i a' chainnt sin?*" Adèle spoke in Gaelic, addressing Inaky. Everyone looked at her.

"Was she speaking that language?" Isabelle asked.

"Yes, it sounded like that. But what language is that?"

"Gaelic."

"And since when do you understand Gaelic, Isabelle?"

"Since your grandmother taught me important phrases for healing, and she also taught me a lullaby to put babies to sleep. I think I have a knack for languages."

"So you were speaking Gaelic last night, Lili."

"But I don't speak Gaelic."

"Well, your ancestors did."

"Isn't it crazy how much you don't know about yourself? But it's exciting to discover it at the same time as you," said Emma.

"It kind of scares me. Not knowing if I'll set something on fire just by snapping my fingers, that's scary," replies Lilou, worried.

"Yes, but at least you can put it out right away," retorted Marc.

They all headed towards the school, walking together with their parents. So, there was no danger in walking there. Lilou was thinking about her speech, and the closer she got to the school, the more nervous she became. A knot formed in her stomach, and her legs began to struggle to support her.

"Evan, could you please help me calm down for my speech? I suddenly feel nauseous. I've never spoken to so many people, especially not for these reasons," said Lilou.

"With pleasure, Lilou. Take deep breaths and look straight ahead. Everything will be fine. You will be extraordinary," reassured Evan.

"How do you know?"

"Because you're already a great queen, and we believe in you. We'll follow you everywhere and always be by your side no matter what happens. We'll always have your back. You'll never be alone," Evan assured her.

"He's right, we'll never leave you alone and be by your side no matter what. I'll talk to the cats so they can pass the message along to everyone," Eva replied.

Nervous and anxious, Lilou looked at Evan and felt incredibly calm in the blink of an eye. My power is truly astonishing. I don't know my powers, and I don't know what I can do and how strong I am. Could I hurt a friend trying to stop a servant of Hades? Could I do something without full control and end up killing a family member? I'm so afraid of not understanding my strengths.

"All the cats have been requested, and they're relaying the message right now to everyone," said Eva, who was running back from the back of the yard, where she was talking to Ziny. A few cats followed her to hear what our future great Queen had to say.

"Thanks, Eva. There are already a lot of people. The message needs to be spread quickly."

Nervous, Isabelle asked, "Do you want me to come up with you, Lilou?"

"No, thanks. Evan will come to calm me down at the same time. But stay close so I can see you. I think it'll help to know a familiar face is nearby."

"I'll be right in front of you."

"Everyone is here, and the speakers are on," said Mathieu.

Lilou took a deep breath, holding Evan's hand as calm settled in her stomach. Checking if the microphone was working well, she gently tapped it with a finger and saw her friends in front of her, parents and grandparents too.

"Thanks to everyone for coming so quickly. Sorry for interrupting a class or training, but I believe my speech is crucial for what awaits us in the coming weeks." She took another deep breath and glanced at Evan. He understood she wanted him close and not to stray far. She needed support. It felt a bit awkward that it wasn't Inaky with her right now, but Inaky nodded, signaling he understood. Evan was the one Lilou needed most at this moment. It wasn't about feelings but necessity. He sent a wave of reassurance to Lilou, and she began her speech.

"How will we defend ourselves with students who aren't adequately trained for this kind of combat? Like me, mostly children. Or with grandparents too old to fight, but who would never allow the young ones to go first?"

"Young people must take over after the fight to rebuild and create a new life," the elder said. "To create a new generation, that's what the elders say. To write and tell the story. All of this must be taught, starting from birth to the next generation. To always be ready for any eventuality."

"What we didn't do for this generation, mine, ours, that our parents protected too much and kept in ignorance." She glanced at her father. "This is what it served you to want to give a real life to your young ones and keep them away from the truth. Today, we risk losing all those we love for not having prepared ourselves. These children deserve to survive and not do the same thing as you did with their children."

"We don't know how things will go. But one thing is certain: we must absolutely close the door of hell forever this time."

She paused. "How to achieve that, I don't know. By closing our eyes and asking for mercy for our protection, for all of us."

"We've worked very hard to be well prepared, but will we be prepared to face the adversary?" She continued, "This adversary whose sole purpose is to eliminate us, to annihilate us forever completely. How will the children react face to face with death? A certain death for many."

"It's hard to think that I was in my room with pink and turquoise walls a few months ago, lying in my bed, breathing my neighbor's lilac scent. And today, in a few days, weeks, I have to try to stay alive by fighting the King of Hell. Hades."

"Until a few months ago, I was just an ordinary 16-year-old teenager. With normal teenage problems and questions that a 16-year-old girl asks herself. Would I have breasts? Will boys find me pretty? Who will be my first kiss? What will it be like?'

'Will I kiss well? Who will ask me to come to prom? Will someone ask me? Etc...'"

"And today, at 17, I have to deal with the fact that my mother isn't dead, as I thought. No, no, and no, not only is she not dead, but she's the Queen of Nature. Which I totally ignored a few months ago. That I am myself, the future queen. I have powers, and some would say they are magnificent. That I live in a world that is not at all the world I grew up in. 'A kind of normal world.'

They say I can conjure fire if needed and find water underground if I'm thirsty. In this world, some men turn into owls, butterflies with women's bodies, and cats that can talk to us and are here to protect us. That I can talk to animals, all animals. Things that haven't happened in centuries. I'm surrounded by friends like:

Mathieu, he can move objects. He can even move a tree and replant it without destroying it.

Emma, who controls the weather. She can make snow in July or summon a hurricane with a snap of her fingers.

Eva, she talks to animals and can also transform into any animal she desires.

Marc, Inaky's cousin, is a man-owl, a swamp owl. He blends into nature. He can also read your thoughts and see what you've seen in the past.

Evan who controls emotions and the atmosphere. He can make you cry when you should laugh or relax you when you're stressed. She turned to him. 'Thank you, Evan.'

Isabelle, my lifelong best friend. She had warrior parents, and we believe she'll be the greatest human shield ever seen.

And, of course, Inaky comes from an owl family but can't transform into an owl. He only has an owl's yellow eyes. So, he can see in the dark as if it's daylight. He can become completely transparent and hide in a room to listen to a conversation without anyone noticing. He can also read minds.

But even with all this and everyone else in our generation, will we be ready to face Hades and his big army? What does he have besides Cerberus by his side to confront us? Even if we lose many people in this war, their sacrifices must ensure his destruction forever. We must be prepared. We will be ready. Hades will be ready too, with his sacred battalion from hell and his three-headed dog. He's been preparing forever. I imagine that he won't miss his chance to rule over the earth this time. He'll have no mercy. Even if he's never had any before, he won't have more now, even less, even if spies are here for him. Please go tell him that Lilou and her entire extended family are ready and that he'll be imprisoned forever in Hell."

Everyone started applauding and shouting, "We will be victorious, we will be victorious." "We have faith in you, Lilou. We are ready to die for the cause. We must eradicate Hades once and for all." And the people shouted louder and louder. "Lilou, Lilou, LILOU, LILOU..." Evan raised Lilou's hand to the sky. With his fingers, he formed an 'L' and shouted Lilou as a sign of respect. And everyone followed suit. They all made an 'L' with their fingers and raised their arms towards the sky, shouting, "Lilou."

The people came to congratulate her for her speech. And to confirm, they would all be ready to face the king of hell. Her parents came and took her in their arms, holding her very tightly.

"You are a great lady, my dear. Your speech was truly sensational. You will be, and you are a great Queen."

****

The weeks that followed were increasingly grey. Fear, despite themselves, settled in each and every one of them. Lilou had asked Evan not to calm anyone down; she wanted people to feel things as they were. The true feelings that often help us react better.

"I believe, no,... I know, that some of us will not return from this war. I really prefer not to know in advance who. But I think it is important to have real feelings at this moment. And to understand well what is happening to us."

"Yes, fear can also be a very good adrenaline and it can be helpful to some people. Sometimes, we have better reflexes when we are afraid or stressed. Others react poorly, they will shrink back or freeze in place, but generally, fear is good adrenaline," replied Evan.

The elderly, pregnant women and children too young to face this war said goodbye to their family and friends. A big dinner and a farewell party were held in their honor because they were the future living generation of our world. Those who would rebuild our world after.

These children are our future generation, the future teachers, parents, and storytellers of their memories. Those who will tell our story. Those who will take care of those who will remain. Injured, half-dead for some. Those who will have seen our parents, friends, sisters, and brothers leave. Those who will have difficult memories to share or even keep in mind. Nothing will be easy and beautiful that day. The future will be tough, and it will be up to them to survive it.

Lilou went onto the big stage, where singers took turns to entertain the evening. She asked the musicians to give her two minutes.

"Good evening everyone. I ask for a little moment of your attention. I want to say a few words before this great evening ends. I would like to thank all those leaving us tonight or in a few days. Those who are the grandparents who gave life to those who will fight in the coming weeks. The future mothers who have in them the future generations that will bring our people back to life after this war. To the children, so small." Lilou had tears streaming down her cheeks. She looked at Evan and signaled to him that she wanted to feel every emotion. It's too important right now to feel everything. "So small and innocent. You are our future. Some may not see their parents again, but you are in good hands. You are already stronger than we were. You will be a great generation. It is you who will ensure that our people remain alive and survive after the war. They will take care of us, those who will remain alive from this war. Injured and emotionally wounded. They will also teach and continue the knowledge and history of what will have taken place here. Ensure that the missing ones are never forgotten. And that this story will be told and taught in future schools as an example to follow. Teach your children how to defend themselves well and be ready for any eventuality. They must know their strength from day one. I don't have the right words to just say thank you! I don't know what to say to tell you how much I love you and thank you for what you do or will do for all of us.

However, I can tell you this: I will not let anyone die whom I could save. We all know that I cannot save everyone, but I will not let anyone die if I can save them. I will always be the first to step forward to protect you and your families. I sincerely hope that we all survive and succeed in eliminating them all. Most importantly, I want to close and seal this door forever, so that it is never reopened. EVER!! I will give my life for this time to be the last. I can swear to you on my life." Everyone stood up and shouted together.

"TO VICTORY!"

"YES TO VICTORY!"

Everyone shouted loudly in unison. The celebration continued until very late that night. People came to hug Lilou and thank her for taking care of their families. An old lady approached Lilou.

"We understand very well the stakes of this war. We also know that many of you will not return. But we are certain that everyone will fight with all their might until the end to save as many people as possible. And above all, to succeed once and for all in locking away this horrible thing deep in hell."

The lady hugged Lilou and kissed her forehead. "I will pass on all my knowledge to the future guardians of these people until my last day. I sincerely hope to have enough time to see you return from this war, and I thank each and every one of you. This is not the first war I have gone through, fortunately, or unfortunately, depending on how we see things. I have always come back, sometimes alone among those with me. I know what it's like to have to leave loved ones behind or to come back without the loved one. To have to go tell a family that the four people they are waiting for will not return. But, at 101 years old, I ask only one day at a time. And to die in my sleep and for my Alfonse to be the one who will come for me. But I promise to take care of your people, as you will take care of mine until the end."

She hugged Lilou tightly and shed a tear in her hair.

To be continued in volume 2...

www.ingramcontent.com/pod-product-compliance
Lightning Source LLC
Chambersburg PA
CBHW070421310726
48977CB00003B/782